‘I came to tell you, Mr Fabbrini, that you have a child. A daughter. Her name is Nicola.’

The silence stretched between them as agonisingly taut as a piece of elastic, then he laughed with incredulous disbelief.

‘So, Miss Nash, I’m a *papa*! You must have harboured the strange notion that I was some kind of gullible fool!’

‘Caroline fell pregnant two weeks before you split up,’ Julia informed him in a stony voice. ‘You can choose to believe it or not, but it’s the truth, and that’s what I came to say. I felt that you ought to know the existence of your daughter. I’ve said what I had to say. I tried.’

She proudly made her way through the crowd when his voice roared through the room, stopping conversation, killing laughter.

‘Get back here!’

Cathy Williams is a Trinidadian and was brought up on the twin islands of Trinidad and Tobago. She was awarded a scholarship to study in Britain, and came to Exeter University in 1975 to continue her studies into the great loves of her life: languages and literature. It was there that Cathy met her husband, Richard. Since they married Cathy has lived in England, originally in the Thames Valley but now in the Midlands. Cathy and Richard have three small daughters.

Recent titles by the same author:

THE RICH MAN'S MISTRESS
SECRETARY ON DEMAND
MERGER BY MATRIMONY

RICCARDO'S SECRET CHILD

BY
CATHY WILLIAMS

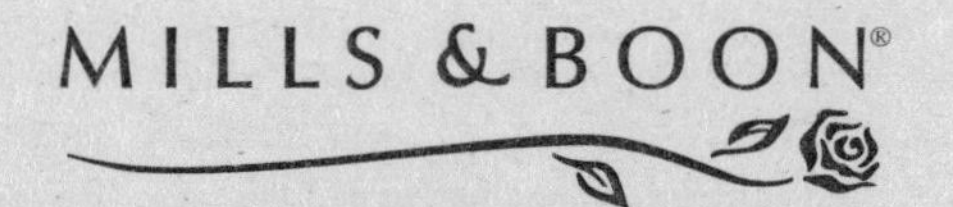

First published in Great Britain 2002
Harlequin Mills & Boon Limited,
Eton House, 18-24 Paradise Road, Richmond, Surrey TW9 1SR

ISBN 0 263 82956 1

Set in Times Roman 10½ on 12 pt.
01-0802-52810

Printed and bound in Spain
by Litografia Rosés, S.A., Barcelona

CHAPTER ONE

RICCARDO FABBRINI stood towards the back of the dim, overcrowded bar, his black eyes narrowed as they moved methodically through the room. He felt another swell of intense irritation hit him as he realised the disadvantage of his situation.

The call had come this morning and the voice at the other end of the phone had been persuasive enough to bypass the rigid series of obstacles that siphoned off all but the most important callers. He hissed an oath under his breath as he continued to scour the room, seeking out the lone female, the woman who had left the message to meet him at an appointed time in this smoky wine bar. If he had personally handled the call he would have made sure to have found out what the hell this meeting was all about. In fact, if he had handled the call there would have *been* no meeting, but Mrs Pierce, competent to the point of meticulousness, had obviously been conned by a soft voice and a fairy story.

Whatever she had to say, it must be good, he thought grimly. It had *better* be good. He was not a man who found it amusing to have his time wasted.

'May I help you, sir?'

Riccardo's dark, impatient gaze focused on a small woman dressed in a waitress's uniform standing next to him, peering up at him, her oval face tinged with pleasure.

He was used to this kind of reaction from the opposite sex and normally he would have automatically fallen back on his charm and flirted with the pretty little thing hovering with her tray tucked neatly under one arm, but this was not a normal situation. He had been manoeuvred into coming here by some woman who had only conveyed to Mrs Pierce that her message was of the utmost importance, relying, no doubt, on his curiosity to grab at the mysterious carrot that had been dangled provocatively in front of his eyes.

Just the thought of it made him catch his breath in another surge of frustrated anger.

'I'm meeting someone,' he answered in a clipped voice.

'What's the name?' The petite blonde moved three steps to a desk at the side and picked up a sheet of paper on which were listed a series of names, most with ticks alongside them, customers who had arrived to take up their reservations.

'That's the one.' He pointed at a name on the sheet, Julia N., with the tick alongside it. 'She's here, is she?' he said grimly, casting his eyes around the room again and failing to find anyone matching up to the woman he had mentally conjured up.

Because conjured her up he had. He would have gone out with her at some point, of that he was sure, which hardly narrowed his options, but he knew his preferences. She would be tall, leggy, blonde and, he had to admit, fairly lightweight in the brains department. That was the way he liked them. Their vanity was his protection from emotional involvement. They enjoyed being seen on his arm, relished the privileges he could offer them but understood their place. Emotional baggage, he had discovered to his cost, did not sit easily on his shoulders.

He also had a good idea of what the woman in question would be after. Money. Weren't they always? However simpering and ingenuous they appeared, his vast bank balance never failed to impress. And he also knew how he intended to deal with any gold-diggers, whatever their trumped-up sob stories. Ruthlessly.

He bit back his anger at finding himself engineered into a meeting he had not initiated and decided, grimly, that now that he had found himself here he would enjoy the situation for what it was worth.

'Just follow me, sir.' The little blonde with the curly hair and the very cute behind walked in front of him and he followed, curious, now that he had come this far, to see where she was leading him. Riccardo anticipated, with a certain amount of relish, a short, sharp and illuminating conversation. Illuminating for the woman in question. Illuminating enough for her to realise that no one, but no one, got the better of Riccardo Fabbrini.

His sensuous lips curved coldly into a smile of anticipated victory.

He was still feverishly scanning the crowd for the single, blonde female, when he realised that his brief tour of the wine bar, which had taken them from the bustling front to a slightly quieter section at the back, had come to an end. He found himself in front of a table at which was seated a slender, mousy-haired woman who had half risen to her feet and appeared to be holding out her hand in greeting.

'May I get you a drink, sir?' enquired the waitress.

Riccardo ignored the polite question and stared in disbelief at the figure in front of him, who had now subsided back into her chair, though she continued to watch him. Very cautiously indeed. As though he might very well bite.

Who the hell was she?

'Mr Fabbrini?' Julia stared up at the towering, olive-skinned stranger and nervously tried to gather herself, already regretting her decision to meet him, even while she knew that the meeting was as inevitable as the sun rising and setting. Inevitable and every bit as difficult as she had imagined it would be, judging from the expression on his face.

'Would you care to sit down?' Julia persisted politely, her anxious eyes briefly meeting those of the waitress, whose expression was sympathetic.

'No, I would not like to sit down. What I *would* like is for you to tell me who you are and why you have wasted my time dragging me here.'

Julia felt clammy perspiration break out over her body like a rash. She took a deep, steadying breath and reminded herself that the man in front of her, menacing though he seemed, could do absolutely nothing to her.

The waitress, having hovered indecisively for a few minutes, had retreated to safer waters, clearly intimidated by him.

'I did think about coming to see you at your office,' Julia said weakly, 'but I decided that a neutral zone might be better. I really wish you'd sit down, Mr Fabbrini. It will be impossible holding a conversation with you if you continue to glare down at me like that.'

'Is this better?' Instead of sitting down, Riccardo leant forward, hands firmly planted on the table so that his eyes were on her level and provided Julia, up close, with a vision of such disconcerting masculinity that she flinched back, an automatic response to his aggressive invasion of her space.

Of course, she knew what he looked like. She had seen pictures of him, and she had heard all about his terrifying personality, but nothing had prepared her for the impact of it full-on. Nothing had prepared her for his height, his overpowering maleness that had her breath catching uncomfortably in her throat, the constricting force of his swarthy good looks.

'No,' Julia said as calmly as she could. 'No, it's not, Mr Fabbrini. You're doing your best to threaten me and it won't work. I won't be threatened by you.' Thank goodness she had made sure that their table was situated at the back of the wine bar, where they were at least out of the range of curious ears and eyes. Thank goodness she had chosen somewhere large and very lively, where this little scene was lost amid the babble of voices and the roars of laughter from the groups of after-work men lounging on stools by the bar.

Riccardo continued to look at her without saying a word. Her smoky voice, so at odds with her average appearance, was controlled and self-contained but her hands were trembling. There was nothing her body could do about containing the effect he was having on her, he thought with a hot stab of satisfaction, even though she was doing her best to quell it.

He pulled out his chair and sat. 'My personal assistant said you refused to supply a surname. I don't like mysteries and I don't like women who mistakenly think that I am gullible enough to be taken in by sob stories or fairy tales. You got me here, and now that I'm here you will give me a few answers. Starting with your name. Your full name.'

'Julia Nash.' She waited to see whether he would react, but he didn't. She hadn't been certain whether he would have recognised the name, but Caroline must have kept it to herself after she had made her grand confession all those years ago. Even in the throes of her emotional distress, she had been quick-witted enough to foresee possible consequences.

'The name means nothing to me,' he said dismissively. He inclined his body slightly to catch their waitress's eye, which seemed remarkably easy. She had removed herself physically from the scene of the action, but had remained at a close distance, fascinated by the strikingly commanding man in his impeccably tailored grey suit. As if an outward show of civilised dress could disguise the primitive male beneath. What a joke, Julia thought.

'Nor,' he continued, after he had ordered a whisky on the rocks, 'have I ever met you before in my life.' He had leaned back into his chair but his presence was still as unsettling as when he had been looming over her.

Riccardo had delved into his memory banks and could state that without fear of contradiction. The name meant nothing to him, even though his antennae had sensed her fear that it might have, and he certainly would have recognised her, if only because she would have stuck out like a sore thumb amidst the parade of beautiful blondes who littered his life.

He took his drink from the waitress without even bothering to glance in her direction, instead choosing to focus his unremitting attention on the woman sitting across the table from him.

'Can I get either of you something to eat?'

'I doubt I will be here long enough,' Riccardo said, briefly looking at the waitress, who nodded in utter confusion at her abrupt dismissal.

'How do you know you haven't met me before?' Julia asked, clutching cravenly at any postponement to what she had to impart, and his lips curled into a coldly speculative smile.

'I have never been attracted to little sparrows,' he drawled, knowing that his uncalled-for and cunningly placed attack had a lot to do with the residue of anger lingering inside him.

That stung, but Julia refused to allow her hurt to show. She would also refuse to allow her loathing for the man sitting in front of her to show either. Loathing that had been already formed by the opinions she had made about him from what she had heard.

'You can be reassured that little sparrows find vainglorious hawks equally unappealing,' Julia said with a tight smile.

'So, now that we have done away with the pleasantries, why don't we just get down to business, Miss Nash? Because business is what you have in mind, is it not?' He rested his elbows on the table and swallowed back the remainder of his drink. 'Perhaps you mistakenly thought that an unusual approach might reward you with a job in one of my companies? If so, then I regret to inform you that I am not a man who favours the unusual approach, especially when it encroaches on my limited and hence very valuable personal time.'

'I'm not after a job, Mr Fabbrini.'

The hesitation was back in her eyes. Through thick black lashes he continued to observe her barely concealed nervousness, the way her slim fingers tried to find refuge in clasping her glass, cradling it, using it as something to steady her apprehension.

Very few things in life evoked Riccardo Fabbrini's curiosity. His meteoric rise through his father's ailing firm had been achieved through cold, calculated hard-headedness and a logical ability to scythe through problems. Curiosity was an emotion that deflected from his sense of purpose and nothing in his adult life had had much power to arouse it.

Even women were as predictable as the ocean tides, despite their reputation to the contrary.

Now, though…

The little sparrow in front of him was stirring something in him. Certainly nothing of a sexual nature, although, behind those prim little spectacles, her eyes were an unusual shade of grey and her body wasn't bad, for someone who could do with putting on a bit of weight. Especially around the bust. And her voice. No wonder Mrs Pierce had been taken in. He was almost looking forward to whatever outrageous lie was hovering behind those delicate lips.

'Money, then,' he said carelessly. 'Are you some kind of charity worker? Mission: hunt down prospective bank balances and tout for donations? If that's the case then make an appointment with my secretary. I'm sure something could be arranged.'

'It's not as easy as that.'

Riccardo was almost disappointed that he had guessed correctly and that money was at the root of this ridiculous charade that had forced him to cancel a date with his latest blonde bombshell. Although, to be perfectly honest, the blonde bombshell was due to be cancelled anyway. Regrettably. She had overstepped boundaries which he himself was only vaguely aware of imposing.

'I beg to differ, Miss Nash. It seems a simple equation and not one that called for this level of subterfuge. You want money, I have money. Just tell me the cause and you'll find that I can be generous with my donations.' He pushed back his chair at an angle so that he could cross his legs and draped his arm over the back of the chair, glancing around him.

'There's no equation to be worked out.'

Riccardo glanced at her. 'No equation? Then tell me what you want and let's get this over with. As I said to you, I am not a man who appreciates mysteries and this one is outstaying its limited welcome.'

Julia paled, realising that retreat was no longer an option. Had never really been an option, although there had always been the illusion of one. But how was she going to phrase what she had to say? She was a teacher. She should have had a thousand words at her disposal, but none that catered for this particular reality. Unfortunately.

She lifted her eyes bravely to look at him and was overwhelmed by the dark, brooding intensity of his gaze.

'It's about your wife. Your ex-wife. Caroline.' She watched as the darkly handsome contours of his face stilled. When he made no response, Julia took a deep breath. 'I thought you might have recognised my name,' she said quietly. 'Well, *Nash*. I thought you might have recognised my surname. But Caroline must not have ever told you...'

Surprises are always unpleasant. Riccardo could remember his father telling him that, many years ago, when the biggest surprise of his life had heralded the receivers coming into his company.

This surprise, though, left him winded. Caroline was the memory he had put behind him, buried beneath other willing women and only seeping out in the angry thrashing of his nightmares. And even those had disappeared.

'Aren't you going to say anything?' Julia's anxious eyes met his and he summoned up all the will-power at his disposal, which was considerable, to maintain his cold, unshaken exterior.

'What is there to say?' he rasped tautly. 'I have no intention of having a cosy chat to you about my ex-wife. May she rest in peace.' He began to stand up and one slender hand reached out, touching him lightly on his forearm.

'Please.' Julia's voice was gentle. 'I'm not finished.'

Riccardo looked at the offending hand with distaste, but remained where he was, locked into place by the viletasting surge of memories that had risen unbidden from deep inside, like ghouls breaking through the barriers of the earth to roam freely.

Julia had half risen from her chair. Now she sat back down and was relieved when he did as well, though not before he had ordered another drink and wine for her, even though she had not asked for any.

'Why should I have recognised your name?' His voice was flat and hard, like the expression in his eyes.

'Because,' she faltered, 'because my brother was Martin Nash. The man who…who…'

'Why don't you say the words, Miss Nash? The man *who replaced me.*' His mouth twisted into lines of bitter cynicism. 'And to what do I owe the pleasure of this trip down memory lane? From what I recall, she was a very wealthy divorcee when we finally parted company. She and her lover. So, did they thoughtlessly not see fit to leave you in their will when they died?' His voice was an insulting mimicry of sympathy and Julia's back stiffened in a flare of rage.

This man was every bit as bad as Caroline had described. Worse. Julia felt a trace of sympathy for the decision her sister-in-law had made. To break off all contact. To say nothing. At the time she had done her best to persuade her otherwise. Through all those shared confidences she had had to steel herself against the unquiet feelings in her heart that a momentous decision was just morally wrong.

Had she known the true nature of the beast, perhaps she wouldn't have made quite such an effort.

'I loved my brother, Mr Fabbrini. And I loved Caroline as well.' Her voice sounded unnaturally still.

Riccardo felt such rage at that admission that he had to clench his hands into tight balls to stop them doing what they wanted to do. His eyes were blazing coals, however, and Julia could feel them burning her skin, searing through her head like knives of scorching steel.

'In which case, please accept my condolences,' he sneered coldly.

'You don't mean that.'

'No. I don't, and I am quite sure you can understand why. You might have loved my ex-wife. You might have seen her as the paragon of beauty and gentleness that she convincingly portrayed, but she was neither so gentle nor was she so compassionate that she couldn't conduct a rampant affair with another man behind my back!' His voice cracked like a whip around her, causing a group of people at the nearby table to glance around in sudden interest at the explosive scenario unfolding in front of them.

'It wasn't like that,' Julia protested with dismay.

'It hardly matters now, does it,' he said in a dangerously soft voice. 'It was five years ago and life has moved on for me. So why don't you just get to the point of all of this and then leave? Go and find a life to live. If you imagine that you are going to find a sympathetic listener in me then you are very much mistaken, Miss Nash. Any feeling I had for my dearly departed ex-wife dried up the day she told me that she had been seeing another man and was in love with him.'

'I haven't come here searching for your sympathy!' Julia retorted.

'Then why *did* you come here?'

'To tell you that...' The sheer magnitude of what she was about to say made the words dry up in her throat. She removed her spectacles and went through the pretence of cleaning the lenses, her hands unsteady on the wire rims.

Without her glasses, she looked wide-eyed and vulnerable. But Riccardo wasn't about to let himself feel sympathy for this girl. The mere thought that she was his replacement's sister was enough to fill his throat with bile. He could imagine her sitting down in a cosy threesome, nodding and listening to their vilification of him, ripping him apart when he hadn't been there to defend himself.

He finished his second drink and was contemplating a

third, which might at least blunt the edge of his mood, when she replaced her spectacles and looked at him. He decided that he wasn't going to help her. Let her stutter out the reason for this bizarre meeting.

'Caroline and my brother had, well…had been seeing each other for the last four months of your relationship before it all came to a head.' The wine had arrived and Julia gulped down a mouthful to give herself some much-needed Dutch courage. 'But they hadn't been sleeping together.'

Riccardo gave a derisive snort of laughter. 'And you believed them, did you?'

'Yes, I did!' Julia's head snapped up in angry rebuttal of his jeering disbelief.

'Well, I may be a little more cynical than you, Miss Nash, but I could not imagine a man and a woman, both in their prime, spending four months holding hands and whispering sweet nothings into each other's ears without the whispering turning to lovemaking. My ex-wife was remarkably beautiful and highly desirable. I doubt if your brother could have kept his hands to himself even if he had wanted to!'

'They never slept together,' Julia repeated stubbornly. That was what Caroline had told her and Julia had believed every word. It had had nothing to do with sexual attraction and everything to do with the man studying her blackly from under his brows. Caroline had been afraid of him. She had confided that to her over and over in the beginning, and the truth of what she had confided had been plain enough to read on her beautiful, pained face.

Riccardo Fabbrini had terrified her. During their brief courtship, she had seen his dark, brooding personality as exciting, but the reality of it had only sunk home once they had married and she had become suffocated by the sheer explosive force of it. Nothing in her sweet-tempered reserves had equipped her to deal with someone so blatantly and aggressively male. The more dominant he became, the less she responded, wilting inside herself like a flower deprived of essential nutrients, and the more she wilted, the more dominant he had become, like a raging bull, she had whispered, baffled by her tongue-tied retreat.

Martin, with his conventional, unthreatening good looks and his easy smile and shy, compassionate nature, had been like balm to her wounded soul.

But they had not slept together. The thought of physical betrayal had been abhorrent to her. They had talked, communicated through those long, empty evenings when Riccardo had taken himself off to his penthouse suite in central London, nursing his frustration in ways, Caroline had once confessed, she could only shudder to imagine.

'Perhaps not,' he now conceded with a curl of his beautiful mouth. 'She did have a bit of a problem when it came to passion. So is this what you came here for? To make your peace with the devil and clear your brother's name now that he can answer only to God?' He laughed coldly. 'Consider it an effort well-done.'

Julia drew in her breath and shivered. 'I came to tell you, Mr Fabbrini, that you have a child. A daughter. Her name is Nicola.'

The silence stretched between them as agonisingly taut as a piece of elastic; then he laughed. He laughed and shook his head in incredulous disbelief. He laughed with such unrestrained humour that the group of eavesdroppers decided that whatever had been brewing had obviously been nothing or else jokes wouldn't have been cracked. Eventually his laughter died, but he continued to grin and this time there was a trace of admiration in his expression.

'So, Miss Nash, I'm a *papa*. I thought you had come for

money, but I confess I was having a little difficulty knowing what platform you would stand on to get it. Now I know and I take my hat off to you. It is the most ingenious platform imaginable. Except for one small detail. You obviously have not catered for my personality. You must have harboured the strange notion that I was some kind of gullible fool, that you could produce your brother's offspring from behind your back and I would fall for it.' He laughed again, but this time there was no humour in his laughter and his black eyes, when they raked over her, contained no admiration. Only distaste.

'Caroline fell pregnant two weeks before you split up,' Julia informed him in a stony voice. 'You can choose to believe it or not, but it's the truth, and that's what I came here to say. I don't want any money from you, but I felt you ought to know the existence of your daughter. It looks as though I made a mistake.'

She stood up, her head held high, and reached for her bag next to the chair.

'Where do you think you are going?' Having coerced him here against his will, the blasted woman was now about to sally forth with her nose in the air, leaving him sitting at a table, nursing a thousand questions which refused to surface. He did not for one minute believe that he had fathered any child, but now that the seed had been planted he intended to get to the bottom of it and force her to confess that she had made the whole thing up.

'I should never have come here, but I felt I had to. I said what I had to say. I tried.' She proudly made her way through the crowd and was on the verge of acknowledging that she was about to make her escape, when his voice roared through the room, stopping conversation, killing laughter and compelling every head to turn in his direction.

'Get back here!'

Julia didn't look back. She did begin to walk more quickly, though, breaking into a slight run as the exit came into sight, then, once outside, she was running, with the wind bitingly cold against her face and rain slashing down on her head. The pavements were slick and empty and she only slowed her pace because there was the very real possibility that she would fall ingloriously on her face in her heels. They were sensible-enough shoes but by no means the sturdy wellingtons she would have needed for the sudden torrential downpour.

She was concentrating so closely on her feet, her head bowed against the driving rain as she scuttled towards the underground, that she was not aware of the sound of footsteps behind her, increasing in speed until she did finally pause, only to find herself whipped around by Riccardo's hand on her arm.

'You walked out on me!' he threw at her furiously.

'I realise that!' Julia shouted back.

'You think you can just show up from nowhere, start talking about my ex-wife and throw some wild story in my face before walking away!'

'I said what I had to say, now let me go! You're hurting me!'

'Good,' he said. 'Some small satisfaction for me for the stunt you pulled back there.'

'Let me go or else I shall yell my head off! You don't want to end up in a police station for assault, do you?'

'You are absolutely right. That is the last thing I want.' He began pulling her behind him while she swatted her hand at his fingers gripping her trench coat.

'Where are you dragging me? You might be able to get away with this caveman behaviour in Italy, but there are laws over here about men who manhandle women!'

'There are also laws against women who think they can blackmail men out of money using a phoney story!'

He was still pulling her and eventually Julia gave up the unequal fight. If he thought he could spirit her away somewhere to prolong their nightmare conversation then he had another think coming. He would no doubt be heading for a cab, and the minute her feet hit the floor of the taxi she would insist on being driven to the nearest underground. She had said what she had come to say, what she had felt morally compelled to say, and if he chose to disbelieve her story then that was his prerogative.

He wasn't pulling her so that he could hail a taxi.

He was pulling her towards his car, a sleek black Jaguar parked discreetly down a side-road.

Julia shied away but he was much bigger and stronger than her and suffused with angry determination.

There was no way that Riccardo was going to let this little madam escape until she confessed that the whole ridiculous thing had been a web of lies.

He realised that he was furiously trying to remember when he and Caroline had made love for the last time. He knew that it was certainly towards the end of their doomed marriage. He had returned home very late and a little the worse for wear with drink, but clutching a bunch of flowers, his attempt to woo the wife who had already mentally left him. The wife, he only acknowledged later, he had already also left behind.

It hadn't worked. She had patiently allowed herself to be awakened, to be presented with the sad bunch of flowers. She had been polite enough to stick them in a vase of water, even though she would surely have been tired at nearly one in the morning. And she had been polite enough to make love, or rather to allow him to make love to her. If nothing else, he had finally realised that it was over between them. But when had it happened…?

'You're lying,' he said harshly. 'And I want you to admit it.'

'I will not get into that car with you.'

'You will do as I say.'

The sheer arrogance of the man left Julia speechless. 'How dare you speak to me like that?'

'Get in the car! We haven't finished talking!'

'I refuse…'

'Why?' he mocked. 'Do you imagine that your womanly assets aren't safe with me? I told you, I don't favour the sparrows.' With which he yanked open the car door and waited for Julia to finally edge into the seat.

She hoped she left a huge, soaking, permanent stain on the cream leather.

'Now,' he said, turning to her once he was inside the car, 'where do you live? I'm going to drop you back to your house and you're going to explain yourself to me on the way. Then, and only then, do we part company, Miss Nash.'

In the ensuing silence Julia seemed to hear the flutter of her own heartbeat.

This was different from when they were in the wine bar, surrounded by people and noise. Locked in this car with him, she became frighteningly aware of his power and of something else: his potent sex appeal, something she had hidden from in the restaurant, choosing to concentrate her mind on the task at hand. The sparrow, she thought in panic, surely couldn't be drawn to the eagle!

'Well?' he prompted with silky determination, and Julia stuttered out her address.

'Not nervous, are you?' He turned on the engine and smoothly began driving towards Hampstead. 'I told you, your maidenly honour is safe with me. Unless…' he appeared to give this some deep thought '…your fear has suddenly kick-started an attack of nerves. Is that it, Miss Nash? Are you afraid of being found out for the liar that you are?'

'I'm not nervous, Mr Fabbrini,' Julia lied. 'I'm just amazed at your arrogance and your high-handedness. I've never encountered anyone like you in my life before!'

'I'm flattered.'

'Don't be!' she snapped back, her body pressed as far against the door as it was physically possible to be. She looked at his averted profile and shivered. Not a man to cross. Those had been Caroline's words and Julia now had no problem in believing them.

'So when did you decide to concoct your little scheme?' he enquired with supreme politeness.

'I haven't concocted anything!'

Riccardo ignored the interruption. The girl was lying, of that he was convinced, and he would break her before the drive was over. Break her and return to his vastly energetic but essentially uncluttered life.

'So…this so-called child of mine is…what did you say? Four? Five?'

'Five,' Julia said tightly, 'and her name is Nicola.'

'And not once did my beloved ex-wife choose to mention this little fact to me. Surprising, really, wouldn't you say? Considering she always prided herself on her high morality?'

'She thought it was for the best.'

Riccardo felt a pulse begin to beat steadily in his temple. Merely contemplating deception of that magnitude was enough to stir him. Just as well none of it was true. He slid a sideways glance at the slight creature sitting in the car, her body pushed against the car door in apprehension. So convincing, but so misguided. The most successful gold-diggers were the ones who hid their intent well.

The girl might not be a stunner, but she could act. She could act because she had brains, he considered. Which would make it doubly satisfying when she finally confessed all…

CHAPTER TWO

THE remainder of the drive was completed in uncomfortable silence. Rain slashed down against the window-panes, a harsh, clattering noise for which Julia was immensely grateful, because without that background din the silence between them would have been unbearable.

Towards the end she gave him terse directions to her house, which he followed without speaking.

By the time the sleek Jaguar pulled up in front of the three-storeyed red-brick Victorian house, her nerves were close to snapping. She pushed open the car door, almost before the car had drawn to a complete stop, and muttered a rapid thank-you for the lift. There was not much else she could thank him for. He had been insensitive, hostile and frankly insulting throughout those tortuous couple of hours in the wine bar. He had refused point blank to believe a word she had told him and had accused her of being a gold-digger.

Julia hurried up to her front door, the rain washing down on her as she fumbled in her bag for the wretched front-door key. She was only aware of his presence when he removed the key from her hands and shoved it into the lock smoothly.

'I want you to tell me what you hoped to gain by spinning me that ridiculous, far-fetched story,' he rasped, following her into the hall and slamming the door behind him.

Julia looked anxiously over her shoulder towards the staircase, which was shrouded in darkness.

And Riccardo, following her gaze, ground his teeth in

intense irritation. She had clung to her fabrication like a drowning man clinging to a lifebelt and he was determined to hear her admit the truth. In fact, hearing her admit the truth had become a compulsion during the forty-minute drive to the house. If not, it would remain unfinished business, even if he never saw or heard from her again, and he was not a man interested in unfinished business.

'I told you...' Her voice was half-plea, half-resigned weariness. Both heated his simmering blood just a little bit more.

'A lie! Caroline would never have kept such a thing from me, whatever her feelings.'

'OK. If you want me to admit that I made up the whole thing then I admit it. All right? Happy?'

Wrong response. She could see that from the darkening of his eyes and the sudden tightening of his mouth. When she had set out on her mission to be honest she had had no idea about the man she would be meeting. She should have. She had heard enough about him over the years, and particularly in that first year, when Caroline had been pregnant and her hormones had unleashed all the pent-up emotion she had managed to keep to herself during her marriage. But time had dulled the impact of her descriptions, and certainly for the past six months Julia had begun to wonder whether her sister-in-law's opinions might not have been exaggerated. Moreover, people changed. He would have mellowed over time.

Looking at his dark, hard face and the ruthless set of his features, she wondered whether anything or anyone was capable of mellowing Riccardo Fabbrini.

'No. No, I am not happy, Miss Nash.' He gripped her arm and leant down towards her so that his face was only inches away from hers. Julia felt herself swamped by him, struggling just to breathe, never mind control the situation.

But her eyes never left his. She was angry and, yes, intimidated, but he could see that inside she was as steady as a rock and he wanted to shake her until the steadiness turned to water.

No woman had ever roused him as much. This was a contest and he sensed that he was losing.

'Come into the kitchen,' she finally said wearily, shaking her arm, which he released. 'I'll explain it all to you, but you'll damned well stop calling me a liar and listen to what I have to say!'

'No one speaks to me like that,' he rasped.

'Sorry, but I do.' Julia didn't give him time to contemplate that assertion. Instead, she turned on her heels and began walking through the dark flagstoned hallway into the kitchen, her backbone straight, refusing to be totally squashed by the powerful man following in her wake.

She could feel him and the sensation sent little shivers racing along her spine. It was a bit like being stalked by a panther, a sleek, dangerous animal that was waiting to pounce.

'Sit down,' she commanded as soon as they were in the kitchen and she had closed the door gently behind them.

This had been Martin and Caroline's house and she wondered whether he would recognise any of the artefacts in the room. Doubtful. Caroline had sold their marital home almost as soon as the divorce had come through and had disposed of the majority of the contents, sending the valuable paintings back to him and selling the rest of their possessions, none of which, she had later told Julia, he wanted. She, along with her lover and every single thing in the house, could go to hell and stay there, for all he cared. The few things she had kept had been little mementoes she had personally collected herself, ornaments and one or two small paintings that had been passed on to her by her own parents when they had been alive.

'Would you like a cup of coffee?'

'This is not your house, is it? Was it theirs?'

Julia looked at him, watched as his shuttered gaze drifted through the room, picking out the homely array of plates displayed on the old pine dresser, the well-worn, much-loved kitchen table with all its scratches and peculiar markings, the faded, comfortable curtains, now blocking out the dark, rain-drenched night.

'Yes, it was. It belongs to me now.'

He began prowling through the room, divesting himself of his jacket in the process and slinging it on the kitchen table. The notice-board, pinned to the wall, was littered with Nicola's drawings. He stared at them for such a long time that Julia could feel the tension searing through her body mount to breaking point. Abruptly she took her eyes off him and began making some coffee.

'Your daughter's works of art,' she said with her back to him.

When she finally turned around it was to find him looking at her, his coal-black eyes narrowed. She took a deep breath and exhaled slowly.

'She started school in September and...'

'Why do you insist on sticking to your ridiculous story?'

Julia didn't reply. Instead, she moved to one of the kitchen drawers and with trembling fingers extracted a photo of her brother, which she handed to him. Martin had been the fair one of them. Even in his thirties, his hair had remained blond, never turning to the mousy brown that hers had. His eyes were blue and laughing.

'That's my brother.'

Riccardo glanced at the picture and very deliberately crumpled it and threw it on the table. 'Do you imagine that

I am in the least interested in seeing what your brother looked like?' he asked in a frighteningly controlled voice. 'I was not curious then and I am not curious now.'

'I didn't show you that picture because I thought you might be interested or curious,' Julia told him. She walked towards the kitchen table and rested his cup of coffee on the surface. She had no idea how he took his coffee but somehow she assumed that it would be black, sugarless and very strong. And she was right. He took the cup, sipped and placed it back on the table, his eyes never leaving her face.

'I showed you the picture so that you could see for yourself how fair Martin was. Almost as fair as Caroline. Of course, he was not nearly as striking as she was, but from a distance they could almost have passed for brother and sister, their colouring was so similar.'

'Where is all this going?'

'I want you to follow me. Very quietly.' She didn't give him time to question her. The more she tried to explain, the more obstinately dismissive he became, the more convinced that she wanted something from him. Money. She would reveal her trump card now and hope that proof of her words would make him see reason.

She put her cup on the counter and began walking back through the house but this time up the dark staircase, pausing only to turn on the light so that she could see where she was putting her feet. For a large man he moved with surprising stealth. She could barely hear his footsteps behind her and, once at the top of the stairs, she turned round just to check and make sure that he was still there. He was. His face grim and set. Julia placed one finger over her lips in a sign for silence and began walking towards Nicola's bedroom.

Her mother, who was already asleep in the guest room,

would have switched on the small bedside light on Nicola's dressing table. Nicola had always been afraid of complete dark. Monsters in cupboards and bogey men lurking under the beds. The stuff of childhood nightmares which no amount of calm reasoning could assuage.

Julia pushed open the door to the room very quietly and went across to the bed and stared down at the child.

Nicola was a living, breathing replica of her father. Her hair, which had never been cut, was thick and long and very black and her skin was satiny olive, the colour of someone accustomed to the hot Italian sun, even though it was a place she had never visited. Her eyes were closed now, but they, too, were dark, dark like her father's, who had joined Julia in contemplation of the sleeping figure.

'You could take a paternity test, but look at her. She's the spitting image of you.'

There was complete, deathly silence at her side, then Riccardo abruptly turned around and began walking out of the room. The sleeping child had aroused sudden, overwhelming confusion in him such as he had never felt before. It had instantly been replaced by rage.

Was it possible to feel such rage? He would have thought not, but he felt it now. Five years! Five years of being kept in ignorance of his own child's existence! His own flesh and blood. Because the minute he had laid eyes on her he had known that the child was his. There could be no doubt.

He thought of his ex-wife and her husband, bringing up *his* child, laughing with *his* daughter, relishing the precious moments of watching those milestones, and his fingers itched with the desire to avenge himself for what he had missed. What had been *his* by right.

He heard Julia running down the stairs behind him and, in the absence of Caroline and her cursed lover, he could feel his body pulsating to unleash his terrible wrath on the slightly built woman following him.

She would have been party to the decision to keep him in the dark about the birth of his child. Whatever her motives for contacting him now, and those motives would surely have something to do with money, she had agreed with the plan to say nothing to him.

He reached the bottom of the staircase and strode into the kitchen. He had to stop himself from smashing things on the way, destroying the contented little nest around him, a contented little nest in which his daughter had been raised. By another man.

Once in the kitchen, he paused and tried to control himself, to regain some of his natural self-composure, which had been blown to smithereens in the space of three short hours.

Somehow he would deal with this. And somehow Julia Nash would be made to pay for the torture she had subjected him to. It mattered not that Caroline and her lover were now no longer around to be held accountable for their vile actions.

Julia Nash was here, accessory to the crime as far as he was concerned, and she would pay the price.

She ran into the kitchen, her face distressed, and he looked at her in stony silence.

'Don't even dare think that you can make excuses for Caroline and what she did! Don't even imagine for one minute that you can justify the immorality of her decision!'

Their eyes locked, Julia helpless to break free from the ice-cold blackness of his stare.

'How dared she think that she could play God and make decisions that would affect my life and the life of my own flesh and blood? And you…' he added in a voice thick with contempt, 'how did you feel watching your brother do the job that should rightfully have been mine?'

'That's not fair!' Julia protested, even though she knew that she was doing little more than shouting in a wind because he was not going to listen to a word she said. But still, she had to defend them both. She might not have agreed with what they had decided to do, but she had been able to see their point. Caroline was terrified that Riccardo, had he known of the existence of his daughter, would do his best to gain custody. The thought of having the fruit of his loins raised by another man would have been anathema to him. So she had silenced Julia's objections. She had reasoned that, however much the courts decided in favour of the mother, Riccardo Fabbrini had the power and the wealth to get exactly what he wanted.

'How dare you talk to me about fair?' he gritted. He slammed his fist on the counter, tipping the edge of the saucer resting beneath her cup, and sent both shattering to the ground. She doubted that he was even aware of it.

'You wouldn't have been married to her!' she persisted, mutinously defying the warning in his eyes. 'You're not comparing like with like. You might have seen Nicola on weekends, but you still wouldn't have shared the completeness of a family home. The marriage was over well before she was born. Before she was conceived, even!'

Riccardo refused to hear the sense behind what she was saying. He felt like a man who had suddenly and inexplicably had the rug pulled from under his feet and in the process found himself freefalling through thin air off the edge of a precipice. No, reason was the last thing that appealed.

The small brown sparrow in front of him might be pleading for his understanding, but understanding was the least emotion accessible to him right now.

'Now that you know, we need to talk about Nicola, decide how often you want to see her.' Julia spoke even though her mouth felt dry, and she had to move to the kitchen table and sit down, because her legs were beginning to feel very uncooperative.

She sat down and ran her fingers through her thick shoulder-length hair, tucking it nervously behind her ears. This meeting had all gone so very wrong that she had no idea where anything was heading any more. She had expected a more civilised reaction, a more accommodating approach. She knew that he was a force to be reckoned with in the world of business. She had reasonably deduced that, that being the case, he would respond with the efficient detachment which would have been part and parcel of his working persona. She had not banked on his natural passion, which now flowed around him in invisible waves, putting paid to any thoughts of a reasonable approach.

'A calm, phlegmatic British approach to a problem, is that it? I am supposed to quietly accept years of premeditated deceit with a smile on my face and then get down to visiting rights. Is that it?'

'Something like that,' Julia admitted hopefully.

'I might have been educated in your fine British system, but I am not a phlegmatic British man,' Riccardo informed her icily. 'When it comes to business I may don the clothes of the businessman and speak with the civilised tongue of your country and deal with the savagery of the concrete jungle with cold-headed judgement, but when it comes to my personal life I am a man of passion.'

Julia felt an involuntary shiver of awareness run through her body like an electric shock.

A man of passion. She had seen that for herself and how! *When it comes to my personal life…* The blood rushed to her head as she imagined the personal life he had in mind.

His passion had overwhelmed Caroline. His powerful drive, instead of sweeping her along, had left her flailing. Had it been that way in bed too? Had his passion driven her into a state of numbed frigidity? She imagined that wild, untamed side of him making love, bringing all his suffocating masculinity to bear upon the object of his desire. The picture shocked her with its vividness and for a few seconds reduced her to a state of confusion.

She shook her head, feeling winded. 'Passion won't help us deal with this situation,' Julia said carefully, treading on thin ice. 'Nicola has never met you. She has no idea who you are and she'll be terrified if you suddenly appear on the scene and try to take her over. She's finding it hard enough to come to terms with losing her…' she nearly fell into the trap of saying *her parents* and reined in the instinct at the last moment '…Martin and Caroline. She will need to be approached with gentleness.'

It took supreme will-power not to give vent to the violent host of objections Julia's little speech produced inside him. He could understand her reason, but, like a wounded and raging bull, he simply wanted to strike out.

Had this calmly spoken girl ever felt anything like the hurt searing through his every muscle now? Had she ever felt what it was like to have your world upended through no fault of your own? Because that was how he felt.

This morning he had been in control of his vastly successful life. He had held his dynasty in the palm of his hand and was gratifyingly aware of the sensual magnetism with which he was blessed, and which could draw any woman he wanted to him.

Now he was being lectured to by this seemingly demure but frustratingly obstinate, mousy-haired woman on how to handle a situation the likes of which he had never expected to encounter. Now he was father to a child and a stranger to her as well.

'I need something stiffer than a cup of coffee,' he said abruptly. Julia thought that perhaps she did as well, especially considering that her own cup of coffee lay in splinters on the ground, something she had temporarily forgotten about. She wearily bent down and began gathering the shards of blue porcelain, tipping them into the bin, while he watched her, his face showing his own intense preoccupation with his thoughts.

She was so busy watching him from under her lashes, wondering whether she could second-guess what he would say next, that when the stray splinter of china rammed into her finger it took her a few seconds to register the pain, and only then because of the sight of the blood.

She stood up quickly, holding the injured finger and biting down on her lower lip to stifle the edge of pain. Pain was not a problem, but the blood threatened to bring on a fainting fit.

She hardly expected him to play the knight in shining armour to her damsel in distress, but perhaps it was just part of his nature to take over.

'What have you done?'

'What does it look like? I've cut my finger!'

He took hold of her hand, inspecting the gash left by the shard, and, with a gentleness that took her by surprise, slowly and efficiently pulled out the offending splinter. His hands were steady and assured. Julia felt the warmth of his hand around hers, the slight abrasiveness of his skin, and she stifled a tremor.

'First-aid kit?'

'It's in the… I'll just go and fetch it…'

Instead of releasing her hand, he walked with her to the small utility room, and when she indicated a cupboard to the left he reached up and extracted a cardboard box that was crammed to overflowing with medication of every variety, most of them suitable for young children. He still had her hand in his. Considering what they had just been through and the currents of hostility that had flowed between them, their physical closeness now was like a parody of intimacy.

'*This* is your first-aid kit?' he demanded, and Julia's grey eyes clashed stormily with his.

'Yes, it is. And before you start telling me that it's not up to your high regulation standards, I'd just like to remind you that I didn't ask for your help! I'm quite capable of seeing to a cut finger!'

'You are as white as a sheet. Where are the plasters? All I can see are cough medicines.'

'They're in there somewhere.' She rummaged through the box and extracted a sad-looking packet wherein lay a stack of plasters adorned with brightly coloured cartoon characters. 'Nicola likes *Winnie the Pooh*,' she told him tersely, extracting one of the plasters. 'I'll wash my finger before I put this on.'

There was no need. Before she could pluck it from his grasp, he took her finger to his mouth and sucked. The action was so shockingly intimate that Julia stared at him open-mouthed. His dark head was bent, but he raised his eyes to meet hers. Was he caressing her finger with his tongue? she thought dazedly. No, of course not. Her body appeared to be on fire. Another illusion, she thought, distracted.

'Saliva is the best antiseptic,' he said, finally removing her finger and holding it up to inspect it. 'There, that looks a lot cleaner now. Give me the plaster.'

She handed him the plaster and, still ridiculously shaken, watched while he gently wrapped it around the slither of open skin. The sight of the blood must have destabilised her more than she had thought at first, Julia decided. She had always had a peculiarly strong aversion to blood. That was probably why her breathing was as laboured as if she had just completed a ten-mile marathon.

That was probably why she wasn't even aware of her mother's presence until she said, mildly but inquisitively, 'Julia! What's going on here? Have I interrupted something?'

'No, of course not, Mum.'

Riccardo watched the play of emotion shadowing the fine-boned, pale face through narrowed eyes. Her mother had startled her, that was for sure, but more than that. She had sprung back guiltily. Afraid of what…?

'You've been on a date? I thought you said you were going to the pub with some friends! You never told me you had a young man.' Her voice was full of misdirected pleasure and Julia felt herself reddening.

She should have told her mother what she was going to do, that she was going to contact Nicola's father, but she had kept it to herself, reasoning that she would confess when everything had been settled. If he had not turned up or else had walked away from the problem then there would have been no need for painful explanations to her mother afterwards.

'Mum…' Her eyes flickered resentfully towards Riccardo. 'This is…'

'Riccardo Fabbrini. Nicola's father.' The biting sting of anger resurfaced as he extended his hand towards the small, grey-haired woman standing in the doorway.

'Nicola's father.' Jeannette Nash tentatively took his hand while her eyes flicked past him to search out her daughter. 'I do apologise. I thought…'

'Yes, Mum.' Julia briskly stepped away from Riccardo

and edged past her mother back into the sanctuary of the brightly lit kitchen. 'I know what you thought. I didn't want to tell you that I was contacting Mr Fabbrini, just in case…' Her voice faltered and when she turned around it was to meet his steely gaze.

'Just in case the meeting was unsuccessful,' he expanded coldly on her behalf. 'Just in case I was the sort of man who would walk out on his responsibilities. As your daughter has discovered, I am very far from being that sort of man.'

'I wish you'd told me, Julia,' her mother accused and Julia sighed. 'What were the two of you doing in the utility?'

Julia had always known how deeply her mother had felt about Caroline's deception and, in the absence of all those telling confidences about Riccardo's personality, Jeannette had stifled her instinct to intervene with great difficulty. All she had seen was a brief, loveless marriage born in haste and rued at leisure. Something to be mourned but for which he should never have been punished by the absence of his own flesh and blood.

'Cleaning up a cut finger,' Riccardo answered. He shoved his hands inside his pockets and perched against the kitchen counter, his long legs casually crossed at the ankles.

'Nicola isn't awake, is she?' Julia asked suddenly and her mother shook her head with a smile.

'Sleeping like a log. I only woke up to use the bathroom and then I thought I'd come down here and fetch myself a glass of water. You know how difficult it is for me to sleep these days, my love.' She turned to Riccardo and said, with forthright honesty, 'This must be a very difficult situation for you. I'm so very sorry but, well, I'm glad that you're here now.'

Riccardo found that he couldn't resist the genuine sincerity in the faded blue eyes and he offered a half-smile, the first Julia had witnessed since she had first clapped eyes on him.

'I'll leave you two alone. I'm sure there's a lot that you need to sort out between yourselves.' She bustled over to a cupboard and poured herself a glass of water. 'I shall see you again very soon, Mr Fabbrini.'

'Riccardo. You can call me Riccardo.' His mouth twisted. 'After all, I am a member of the family now.

'Several years too late,' he said softly as her mother left the kitchen. 'But here now, Miss Nash. Are you not thrilled to have accomplished what you set out to do?' He flashed her a bitterly mirthless smile and pushed himself away from the counter.

How many more members of this cosy little unit from which he had been ruthlessly excluded? he wondered. Aunts and uncles in the background? Cousins maybe? A full life just lacking the ingredient of father?

Except, he thought with hard-edged cynicism, Nicola *had* had a father. This woman's brother. The only father she had ever known. She'd called him *Daddy* and sat on his shoulders when they went to the park.

Riccardo's shuttered gaze concealed his white-hot fury. For a few seconds back there, as he had dealt with her finger, he had felt a certain uninvited empathy with her. It hadn't lasted. Nor would it return.

'You said you wanted something stronger than coffee,' Julia said, avoiding his rhetorical question. 'I have some wine in the fridge, but that's about it.'

'As frugal in matters of alcohol as your sister-in-law was?'

'I prefer to keep my head.' Especially now, she thought as she opened the fridge and extracted a bottle of Sauvignon. She could feel his heavy-lidded dark eyes raking over her as she poured them both a glass of wine, his a large glass, which might do something to take the edge off that ferocious fury which she could feel him tightly keeping in check, hers a smaller glass, just enough to cope.

So in control, Riccardo thought, or at least determined to be. Which made her little slip-ups all the more intriguing. She hadn't been in control when he had taken her finger into his mouth. Her body had become rigidly still and he had breathed in her unwilling response to him, to the warmth of his tongue rubbing against the soft flesh of her finger. And then when her mother had surprised them she had been startled. The obvious answer was that she felt guilty to have gone behind her mother's back and contacted him, but there was something else.

He imagined what it would be like for her to see her carefully planned life brought to a standstill, just as his had been.

'Why did you decide to contact me?' he asked, sitting down at the table and pushing back the chair so that he could extend his long legs in front of him. His fingers caressed the rounded contours of the wine glass before he brought it to his lips, sipping some of the wine while he continued to direct his unsettling gaze on Julia's face. 'Would it not have been easier to have maintained the secret rather than risk kick-starting a situation you might end up having no control over?' Here's where the money angle comes in, he thought cynically.

Julia, sitting opposite him, elbows on the table like a child being interviewed, lowered her eyes. 'I did what I thought I had to do,' she said. 'When Caroline was alive I respected her wishes…'

'Because you agreed with her, because you saw nothing wrong in writing off my existence…'

'Because it was what she wanted. Because I loved my

brother and wanted what I thought was best for them both.' Her jaw hardened and she challenged him to try and prolong the probing. 'What we have to deal with is reality. What's happening now.'

Riccardo forced himself to let it go. He was so unused to having to let anything go when his instinct told him to pursue that the withdrawal felt like bile in his mouth. 'For which you no doubt have a plan.'

'I don't think you should tell Nicola who you are to start with…' When his mouth opened in outrage she firmly stood her ground, refusing to back away. 'I know this is hard for you to accept, but I don't think she can cope with too much now. Get to know her and when she trusts you then perhaps you can tell her who you are, tell her that you are her blood father.'

'As opposed to what your brother was, you mean?' His lips curled and she met his eyes evenly.

'That's right. She's always known that Martin wasn't her real father. Neither he nor Caroline pretended to her otherwise.'

'I will come and see her tomorrow. When she finishes school. What time does she get home? Do you bring her home with you? Does she attend the same school where you teach?'

More at home with being the one who answered the questions as opposed to posing them, Riccardo grudgingly acknowledged the shift in emphasis.

'Yes, I teach at her school, but not in the junior section. I teach the older pupils, and I've been leaving school early so that she can come home with me. I do a lot of my work from home now, after school hours.'

Riccardo had a glimpse of her view of things and it irked him to realise that she was due some sympathy as well. Her life had been changed too, though, he reminded himself grimly, not quite to the same extent as his. He finished his wine and refused the offer of a refill. She, he noted, had toyed with hers, barely drinking any.

'We're normally back home by around four-thirty. If you like, you can drop by around five. She should have had her bath by then.'

Riccardo stood up. It had, he conceded, been the longest day of his life. He slung on his jacket while Julia hovered by the table, keeping herself at a distance, he noticed. He wanted to have another look at his daughter, drink in her sleeping face before he left, but no, there would be time enough tomorrow.

'Does your mother live here with you both?' he asked, as they walked towards the front door, Julia virtually sprinting to keep pace with his long strides.

'She has her own place. She was here to babysit.'

'And you? Where did you live?' He paused by the door, frowning at her as he tried to complete the pieces to this jigsaw that had now become a part of his well-ordered life.

'I rented a flat,' Julia told him vaguely.

'This arrangement must have dented your freedom,' he said without the slightest indication of sympathy in his voice, and when she returned his look with a puzzled one of her own he shrugged. 'Men. A five-year-old chaperon can't have been welcome.'

'It hasn't been a problem,' Julia told him stiffly. She yanked open the front door to find that the rain had softened to a steady, bone-chilling drizzle.

'Because there's no man.' Riccardo watched as her face reddened and the defiant shake of her head couldn't quite hide the fact that his offhand assumption had struck home. 'Is that why your *mama* sounded so pleased when she thought you had brought home a date?' He felt a curl of satisfaction as he watched her flounder. He had spent the past few hours floundering. Now it felt good to have the shoe on the other foot, even though the situations could not be compared.

'You're here because of your daughter,' Julia informed him coldly. 'My personal life has nothing to do with you.' The jeering mockery in his eyes sent her reeling back to that secret place where all her insecurities lay hidden, but never in a million years would she let him see that.

'Which suits me,' he countered smoothly, the hard lines of his face accentuated by the play of shadows from the dim front porch light overhead. 'Till tomorrow. And I am warning you, from now, I will not be open to debate on when I see my daughter. You may hold the upper hand at the moment, Miss Nash, but time has a nasty habit of changing things...'

CHAPTER THREE

'HE SEEMS like a nice man, considering.'

'Considering?' Julia finished plaiting Nicola's hair and tugged both ends so that the child swung around to look at her. Her eyes were almond-shaped and probably not quite as onyx-black as her father's, but the thick lashes were the same. *Nice man?*

'Who seems like a nice man?'

Julia and her mother exchanged a look. 'Just someone who's going to be coming around in a little while, honey.'

'Oh. Can I watch cartoons on TV before tea?'

'Not at the moment. In a while, maybe.'

'Considering...' her mother hissed, doing something comical with her eyebrows that would have made Julia burst out laughing if the subject matter at hand had not been quite so grim.

'What's for tea, Aunty Jules?'

'Chicken.'

'I hate chicken. Do I have to eat it?' Nicola stuck her hands in the pockets of her dungarees and made a face.

'Chicken nuggets.'

'I do wish...' her mother began and Julia flashed her a warning glare. 'Well...and he's very handsome.'

Julia, who had spent the day in a state of muted dread, almost found herself wishing that the doorbell would ring. She had been down this conversational route with her mother countless times before, daily, it seemed to her, since Caroline and Martin were no longer around to provide a buffer, and she wasn't about to go down it again.

'Not interested,' Julia hissed, edging her mother away from curious infantile ears. Amazing, she had discovered, what they managed to pick up when you could swear that their concentration was focused firmly on something else. 'I'm fine, Mum. I have my job. I'm perfectly happy. I certainly don't need a man.' And I most certainly don't need a man like Riccardo Fabbrini, she added silently to herself.

'But it would be nice to see you sorted out, Jules. It won't be easy, you know...' her mother's eyes flitted tellingly to Nicola, who was absorbed in drawing a picture, her face a study in concentration *'...bringing up Nicola all on your own.'*

'Mum. Please. Not now. Please? He's going to be here any minute now.'

'And look at you. Old jeans, checked shirt, flat shoes...'

Julia grinned. 'You know me. Twenty-seven going on twelve. It's a reaction to having to deal with nine- and ten-year-olds all day long.'

'Well, darling, that's as maybe, but...'

Fortunately, Julia was not required to hear the end of her mother's predictable sermon on the joys of marital bliss and the sadness of an old woman's heart when her only daughter appeared to be doing nothing about acquiring any of the said marital bliss.

She wiped her clammy hands on her jeans and slowly pulled open the front door.

Riccardo Fabbrini was every bit as daunting as she remembered. One night's restless sleep had not managed to steel her against the reaction she instinctively felt as their eyes met and the force of his aggressive personality settled around her like a miasma.

This time he was not in a suit. Perhaps he had thought that a suit might have been a little offputting for a casual meeting with his five-year-old daughter.

His informal attire did nothing to deaden his impact, however. The cream jumper and dark green trousers only served to emphasise the striking olive tones of his colouring.

'Is she here?' he asked tersely and Julia nodded, standing well back as he walked into the hall, carrying in his hands two large boxes.

'In the kitchen, with Mum.' No preliminaries. He had come, she thought without much surprise, with his hostility firmly in place. It was stamped in the harsh coldness of his face as his black eyes had swept over her. A night's sleep certainly had done nothing for his temper.

'Your mother is here as well? To give you a bit of moral support, Miss Nash? What do you imagine I am going to do? Kidnap my daughter and spirit her away to foreign shores?'

'For her sake, perhaps, you might want to maintain a semblance of courtesy.'

Riccardo nodded curtly. He had taken the day off work, had gone to Hamley's and spent more hours than he would ever have imagined possible to spend in a toy store, looking for the perfect toy. A difficult task, considering he had not the slightest idea what five-year-old girls liked, and now here he was, already being outmanoeuvred by this chit of a woman with her bookish spectacles and neat outfit.

Overnight, his rage had quietened. But only marginally. He had, however, managed to recognise that he would have to play along with her rules for the moment. Whatever his paternal status, Julia Nash knew his child and he didn't. It was as simple as that. The recognition, far from slaying his thirst for revenge, a revenge thwarted as his ex-wife was no longer around, only muted it slightly. The blood that ran through his veins was too grounded in passion to lightly release the past and calmly accept the future without demur.

The kitchen was warm and cosy. That was his first impression as he walked through the door behind Julia. A scene of perfect domesticity. At the kitchen table, Nicola sat with her head bowed over a piece of paper, and Jeannette Nash bustled by the kitchen counter, stirring custard in a saucepan. He felt like an intruder with his packages clutched in his hands.

Jeannette was the first to break the ice, much to Julia's relief. She turned around and smiled, wooden spoon still in her hand.

'Riccardo, how lovely to see you again. Nicola, darling, we have a visitor.'

Nicola looked up from what she was doing and Riccardo felt a wave of unsteadiness wash over him as he looked at the little girl at the table, her dark hair braided away from her face, her dark brown eyes staring back at him with mild curiosity.

'Hello…' This was such new terrain for him, a man normally in command of any situation life had ever been able to throw at him, that he instinctively looked towards Julia, who read the awkwardness in his eyes and felt her heart soften towards the powerful, aggressive man now hovering uncertainly in front of his daughter.

'Nicola,' she said quietly, 'why don't you show Riccardo what you're drawing? He loves art and he's never seen what a talented five-year-old girl can do.' Loves art indeed, she thought wryly. Although, he did, didn't he? The memory struggled out from the dim recesses of her brain, the memory of Caroline telling her that that was one of the first things that attracted her to him. They had met at an art show and he had been deeply and genuinely interested in the pieces, had been able to talk at length and knowledgeably about paintings. She had misread his interest for an insight into a sensitive nature. Time, she had said more than once, had put paid to that illusion.

But he was certainly doing his level best to maintain it as he walked hesitantly towards Nicola and looked at what she was drawing.

'It's an elephant,' she said. 'There's the trunk.'

'Ah, yes. I see.' He moved a bit closer and bent down, nodding. 'Yes. But it is a very fine elephant. Will it have any legs, do you think?'

'Oh, yes.' She drew four sticks. 'There. Legs.'

'Excellent legs.'

Nicola looked pleased with the flattery and smiled, her curiosity a bit more alive now that the man had passed the crucial test of admiring her work.

'Want to keep it?' she asked and he nodded again.

'Perhaps you could write your name under it.' He could feel his skin prickling with nerves and felt another rush of dislike towards the people who had put him in this situation. Behind him, he knew that Julia was looking at him. Mentally ticking off various boxes in her head, he wondered acidly, labelled *Pass* and *Fail*?

'I...I've brought you something. Well, two things actually. Presents.'

Nicola paused with her pencil raised in mid-air and her eyes slid away from Riccardo towards Julia, who smiled weakly. Riccardo gruffly shoved the wrapped parcels towards his daughter and then stood back with his hands stuffed into his pockets.

'You can open them,' Julia said lightly, and Riccardo gritted his teeth together in frustration. To be viewed with suspicion by his own flesh and blood! To have to seek approval from a woman whose brother had crept into his marital bed and seduced his wife!

The woman in question had approached them, moving

to stand next to her niece so that the three of them formed an uneven triangle around the table. Riccardo refused to look at her, refused to give her the satisfaction of seeing his own uncertainty.

Nicola, oblivious to the tension crackling around her and blithely unaware that she was the focus of his intense concentration, began opening the parcels, her face softening into pleasure as she held up the stuffed Winnie the Pooh bear for them all to see, then the little stack of books, which she looked at one by one, turning each over in her hand until Riccardo muttered uncomfortably, 'I wasn't too sure what you liked and what you did not.'

'Thank you very much.' The almond-shaped eyes were now very curious indeed. 'I love them. Aunty Jules can read one to me tonight,' she added politely, her eyes flicking for support from Julia as she became attuned to the undercurrents zinging through the room.

When Jeannette spoke the strange scenario was broken, thankfully, and then, with tea and pudding and the necessary bustling around the kitchen, something approaching normality was achieved.

Jeannette chatted happily to Riccardo, leaving Julia free to say as little as possible by way of direct address, although her eyes drifted back to him with unnerving regularity. She watched the way he sat in the chair, his long fingers curled around the cup of tea her mother had made for him, his lithe body inclined towards his daughter. The kitchen was warm and he had removed his jumper so that now he simply wore a green and white checked short-sleeved shirt that exposed powerful, swarthy forearms liberally sprinkled with dark hair. Everything about him redefined the word *male*. How gorgeous he and Caroline must have looked together, she thought. He was so tall and dark and forceful and she had been just the opposite, small and blonde and exquisitely pretty. Just the sort of woman a man like Riccardo Fabbrini would be attracted to, Julia thought. Not a timid brown sparrow like herself.

She dragged her attention back to what was happening around her and only realised the time when her mother rose to leave.

'Will I see you again?' Nicola asked shortly after Jeannette had left, pausing by the kitchen door with her small hand in Julia's, ready for her routine of bath and bed. 'Are you and Aunty Jules going out together?'

The innocent question hung thickly in the air. Of course Nicola must have wondered what this strange man, whose resemblance to her she had either not noticed or else only subconsciously acknowledged, was doing in the house. And she had overheard her mother insinuating more than once how nice it would be if Julia could find herself a nice boyfriend and think about settling down before all the nice men were snapped up. Nicola had put two and two together and was now asking whether they came to four.

Julia quickly tried to work out how she could disabuse her niece of this notion without her denial leading to other questions, such as why a perfect stranger who was not going out with her had arrived armed with presents for a child he had never seen.

'Yes, we are, as a matter of fact, little one,' Riccardo said smoothly, before Julia could intervene. He countered her shocked look at him with a bland smile that challenged her to refute him. 'We are most certainly going out.' This time the smile sent a chill of apprehension racing down her spine. It was a smile loaded with intent.

'It's time for your bath,' Julia told Nicola in a breathless voice.

'And you'll read me a story?'

'I will,' Riccardo intervened, 'if you would like.'

'I would rather Aunty Jules. She always reads to me now.'

Only Julia caught the grimness of his expression as their eyes tangled, and she shivered. She would let none of her own apprehension show for Nicola to see, and she didn't, but by the time she returned to the kitchen her seething temper at his casual exploitation of the situation was on the verge of reaching boiling point.

She steamed into the kitchen to find him lounging on one of the kitchen chairs, flicking through Nicola's drawing book, with a glass of wine in his hand. He looked up as soon as she stormed in, in no way apparently intimidated by the light of fire in her eyes.

'Would you care to tell me what the hell you were playing at? Telling Nicola that you and I were going out? How dare you?'

'Why don't you go and pour yourself something to drink and calm your frayed nerves?'

His dark eyes were unreadable. Gone was that glimpse of a man no longer in control of his situation. All that hesitation he had displayed in the company of his daughter had vanished. Every inch of him now breathed self-assurance.

Julia wondered how she could have softened towards him, even momentarily. The only drink she wanted to pour was not down her throat but over his arrogant head!

'If my nerves are frayed then you're the reason!' Julia sat down opposite him and his utter composure only served to fire her up more. 'What did you think you were doing, telling Nicola that you and I...that you and I *were going out together*!'

He took his time answering. He inspected the pale gold liquid in his glass, then tilted it to his lips so that he could swallow another mouthful.

'Did you think that you were going to have things all your own way?' he asked softly. 'You suggested that I don't tell my own daughter who I am because it might destabilise her and she is already coping with the loss of her mother and your brother.' He found that he could not bring himself to refer to Martin in any other way. 'I respected that decision, but tell me this…how am I supposed to put in an appearance without her wondering who the hell I am? And why am I showing such a disproportionate interest in her when I am nothing to you?'

'She's five years old! She's hardly going to sit down and analyse the situation!'

'She might be five years old but she is not a fool!' He leaned forward, his mouth a thin line of ruthless determination. 'She was clever enough to ask me exactly who I was! What do you suggest I tell her? The plumber? And I will be back to pay another visit to take care of the leak? Oh, and by the way, I shall return with more presents? Do you imagine that she would have fallen for something like that?'

'I would have thought of something!' Julia snapped back. 'Eventually. When I thought the time was right.'

'Well, perhaps I am not prepared to play your waiting game, Miss Nash. No, *Julia*. Now that you and I are going out together.'

'We are not going out together!' The way he had said her name. Like a caress. It had stolen over her heated skin and something else had thudded through her. It was something Julia had no intention of focusing on. Instead, she rose to her feet, muttering under her breath, and poured herself a glass of wine.

'And by the way,' she ranted, one hand on her hip, the other holding her full glass, 'make yourself at home, why don't you? Just waltz along and help yourself to the drinks!'

Riccardo looked at her and felt his lips begin to twitch into a smile. The picture she presented! All ruffled outrage, cheeks flushed, her rimless spectacles glinting furiously in the light, five foot three of womanly fury. He had seen many women and in many different lights, but this sort of outspoken fury, unrelated to anything sexual, was a first.

'Are you going to sit down and listen to what I have to say or are you going to stand there exploding?'

'Has anyone told you that you, Mr Fabbrini, are an arrogant swine?'

Riccardo carefully considered the question. 'No, but then you might want to remember that perhaps my arrogance has to do with the situation you have thrust upon me.'

Julia muttered again, but sat down and drank a long, soothing mouthful of her wine.

'I have to get to know my daughter. Gradually. For that, I have to have a reason to visit her, if you don't want her to know who I am. What better way to visit on a regular basis than in the guise of your lover?'

Julia felt a steady heat begin to pulse in her veins. His eyes roved lazily over her flushed face.

'That way, I can get to know her. I can be allowed the chance to know my own daughter. To bring her the presents I have been denied the pleasure of doing for five years, to hold her hand in mine, to receive her trust. Because she loves and trusts you and it might make it easier for her to accept me through you.'

His deep, slightly accented voice washed over Julia, filling the corners of her body like incense. She was dimly aware that he was being reasonable.

'And it is not as though I am competing with anyone

else,' he finished smoothly, dipping his eyes so that his long lashes drooped against his cheek. 'Is it?'

'That's not the point,' Julia said stubbornly.

'No, but it makes things a lot easier. It's a nice house,' he said, looking around the kitchen. 'Nothing at all like the house we shared.'

Julia followed his eyes but said nothing. The house he had shared with Caroline had been, according to her descriptions of it, a show home. A place designed for the sumptuous entertaining of important people.

'It's very comfortable and homely,' he mused. 'A family home.'

'Are you surprised?'

'Surprised because Caroline never seemed interested in homeliness. She always preferred the trappings of wealth.'

Julia laughed and he looked at her narrowly.

'Care to share the joke?'

'The joke is,' Julia said sardonically, 'that Caroline hated the trappings of wealth.'

A dull flush crept into his face. He felt like someone on the edge of some impossibly big secret, a secret that everyone knew about but had managed to keep from him. 'According to you,' he said coolly, and Julia raised her eyebrows.

'According to Caroline, actually. She loathed the army of interior designers who spent weeks swarming through your mansion. When she and Martin bought this house she chose everything herself. From the colours of the paint on the walls to the shade of every tie-back in every room. How on earth could you have lived with someone, been married to them, and not have realised that what they truly wanted was a cottage in the country, and if not the cottage in the country then at least an unpretentious family house in the city?'

'I don't appreciate being patronised, *Julia.* You'll have to be aware of that if this relationship of ours is to stay the course.'

'We don't *have* a relationship, as I've already told you. And I'll be as patronising as I like. You might be able to give orders to all your minions, but I'm afraid I'm not open to being ordered about.'

Riccardo carefully placed his empty wine glass in front of him and proceeded to relax in the chair, hands behind his head. He looked at Julia with interest. Funny, but when she was still she gave the appearance of someone serene, something in the calm set of her features and the way she seemed to observe without comment would lead anyone to assume that she was as placid as a lake. But there were times when she spoke and her face was alive with animation. Like now. Like earlier on, when she had stormed into the kitchen, all fire and brimstone.

His eyes dropped from their interested inspection of her face to the swell of her breasts, just visible under the sexless shirt. His interest became somewhat less dispassionate and he straightened up to conceal an inappropriate stirring in his loins.

'Is it any wonder your mother is tearing her hair out at the prospect of you finding a man?' Riccardo drawled, pulling the tiger's tail. He felt a sudden thrill of excitement when she stood up and came across to where he was sitting. She leaned towards him, quivering with aggression, her face pink with anger, hands firmly placed on her boyish hips.

'My mother is not *tearing her hair out at the prospect of me finding a man*,' Julia hissed. 'And I utterly resent you voicing opinions on *my private life*, about which you know *absolutely nothing*! You met me for the first time *yesterday* and *don't you dare* think that you are somehow entitled to *shoot your mouth off* as though you know me. *You don't know me* and you never will!'

'Never say never,' Riccardo informed her silkily. He knew that he was pushing her to the limits of her patience. After what he had been through, that in itself should have been a source of immense satisfaction, but there was something else. He was enjoying her open display of temper. He wondered what she would do if he really gave her something to get worked up about. If he pulled her towards him and kissed her. Covered that angry mouth with his own. He imagined that she would fight him, but then what? Melt? And if she did melt, how would that feel?

'I think it's time you left, Mr Fabbrini.'

'The name is Riccardo. Use it.'

'Or else what?'

'You don't want to lay down any gauntlets for me,' he said softly and watched her grey eyes hesitate as she wondered whether to continue the argument. She backed away, leaning against the kitchen counter, waiting for him to stand up and leave.

'To all intents and purposes, you and I are now an item. Are we not, *Julia*?'

There he went again. Saying her name in that velvety, caressing voice. He was doing it deliberately. Laughing at her. And he talked about *her* patronising *him*!

'If you think it would help you in getting to know your daughter then I shall oblige, but…'

'But…?'

'But don't think that that gives you any rights over me…'

'Rights? What kind of rights?'

Julia didn't know what kind of rights. She knew what she wanted to say but she just couldn't find the words, so she glared impotently at him.

'It's time you left. I have to work tomorrow and I don't want to be late.'

'It's...' Riccardo calmly consulted his watch '...eight-forty-five. Surely not even a primary-school teacher with an over-developed sense of duty could call that late. And what about dinner?'

'What *about* dinner!'

'Perhaps we should have some.' Perversely, now that the object of his visit had retired to bed, instead of rushing to leave, to clear out of the company of this woman whom he had seen from the outset as a conspirator in his ex-wife's plot to deceive him, he wanted to prolong his stay.

Aside from anything else, he had no intention of being seen to be malleable. She might be able to call the shots, *for the time being*, as far as his daughter was concerned, but there her temporary power ended.

'I want to find out about Nicola,' he inserted when she made no move to abandon her mutinous stance by the kitchen counter. 'I know nothing about her and I have a lot of catching up to do.'

'What sort of things do you want to know about?' Julia asked distantly, and he stood up and moved across to her with such speed that she was barely aware of his intent until he was standing directly in front of her, caging her in with his hands, his face dark with sudden anger.

'What do you think? Why don't you use your imagination and figure it out? Pretend for a moment that you're in my shoes. Wouldn't you have just a little shadow of curiosity about your child?'

Julia was finding it difficult to breathe, never mind pretend anything. His face was so close to hers that a sudden movement would involve physical contact of the most disastrous kind.

'All right,' she said weakly. 'I'll...do something for us

to eat and you can ask me any questions you like...' He didn't move and she was formulating a polite way of telling him that cooking was an impossibility while she was being held hostage against a kitchen counter, when he suddenly reached out with one hand and removed her spectacles.

Without them, Julia felt hideously vulnerable. She blinked rapidly. 'What are you d-doing?' she stammered.

Riccardo didn't know what he was doing. He had wanted to see her eyes without the barrier of her glasses. They were a pure shade of grey and without her spectacles concealing them were fringed with thick, long lashes. He stared at them and then abruptly pushed himself away, while she turned and immediately re-armed herself with her glasses.

'When did she start school?' he asked gruffly, sitting back down, shaken by the realisation that he had wanted to kiss that quivering mouth of hers again. He reminded himself that, aside from being on the opposite side of the fence, she was not the sort of woman he was attracted to. 'Does she enjoy it? Does she have friends?'

Julia breathed deeply and began answering his questions while she rummaged in the cupboard for a saucepan and busied herself with chopping mushrooms and onions, efficiently preparing a light pasta dinner for them. Something that could be cooked and eaten within the hour, after which he would have no excuse to stay. His presence in the kitchen was wreaking havoc with her normally very unruffled nervous system and the sooner he cleared out the better.

'And was she happy?' he asked when his plate had been deposited in front of him and he had poured them both another glass of wine. 'Here? With Caroline and your brother? Did she ever ask about me?'

Julia glanced across the table to him. 'I don't know. I

wasn't living under the same roof, so I don't know what questions she asked or didn't ask about you.'

'And you didn't have any thoughts on the matter?' he pressed on mercilessly. 'The three of you were perfectly content to erase my existence? What about your brother? Did he share the same cavalier attitude?'

'We've been through all this,' Julia said tightly.

'And we'll go through it again. Tell me.'

'Caroline felt as if she was caught between the devil and the deep blue sea,' Julia sighed, closing her knife and fork and propping her chin on the palm of her hand. 'You want to make her out to have been without any morals, but she was afraid that if you knew about the pregnancy, about the baby, you would take Nicola away from her. She said that you were fiercely family-oriented, that you came from a big, close family and that the thought of sharing the upbringing of your child with another man would have been unacceptable to you. And Martin loved her. He agreed because he only ever wanted what made her happy. I know you don't want to hear any of this, but you did ask.'

'Was she *that* scared of me?' he asked and Julia hesitated, not knowing whether he really wanted an answer or whether he had just been thinking aloud, turning over the thought in his mind.

'Answer me!' he commanded, which was Julia's cue to spring to her feet and begin clearing away the dishes.

'You frightened her,' she said eventually, her eyes flicking to his own shuttered, brooding gaze. 'Or maybe I should say that you overwhelmed her.'

'And I suppose she lost no time in confiding all these girlish secrets to you?' he asked acidly. 'Instead of confiding in me and trying to make a success of our marriage, she sought comfort in the arms of a stranger and found release in pouring out her problems on any receptive ear she could find, just so long as it wasn't mine!'

'Stop making yourself out to be the angel, Riccardo!' Julia snapped, only realising afterwards that she had called him by his name, conferring an intimacy on the situation between them that she strenuously resisted.

'Oh, but I was the angel,' he said smoothly. 'There were times when I could easily have taken a lover, when the thought of returning to the house and to a wife who made love as though under sufferance would have been incentive enough, but I didn't.'

'What a saint,' Julia muttered under her breath.

'Sorry? I didn't quite catch that.'

'I *said* that I'm feeling rather tired. Do you want to arrange another day for you to come over and see Nicola? I know that she's going to one of her little friends' for tea tomorrow, but perhaps the day after? Or maybe some time on the weekend?'

Riccardo felt a surge of irritation at her diversion tactic, but he swallowed it back and he hid his natural anger at finding his movements dictated by someone else.

'Perhaps Saturday,' he said, 'I can take you both out to lunch somewhere. Where would she like to go?'

'Oh, any place where the meal comes in a box with a toy,' Julia told him with a smile and he grimaced.

'In other words, French food is out of the question.'

'Out of the question,' Julia agreed. She looked at him curiously. 'This must be, yes, I know, very hard for you, but also...very different. Do you have nephews? Nieces?' She stood by the kitchen sink, arms folded.

'Four nephews, all much older. They live in Italy with my two sisters and their husbands. As for nieces, no. But she has a ready-made family, complete with grandmother.' He grimaced wryly and caught Julia's eye. 'My mother is a very assertive woman,' he said, almost adding *a bit like you*. 'But very fair. She has been longing for a *bambina* in the family. Nicola will find herself swamped by her affection.'

'And you've told them about…the situation?'

'Not yet, no. You have your own timescale as to when you think Nicola should be made aware of who I am, and I have mine when it comes to my family.' He stood up and raked his long fingers through his impossibly dark hair while Julia watched him cautiously from a safe distance.

'And what are your…intentions once Nicola knows that you're her father?' Julia asked, taking the bull by the horns. 'The reason I ask is that if you intend to return to Italy to live and take her with you then I shall do my utmost to prevent it.'

'Is that a threat?' he asked mildly, shrugging on his jacket and preceding her to the front door.

'Of course it's not.' Julia wrapped her arms around her body, hugging herself. 'But this is the only life that Nicola knows. To be removed from it…'

'Would require a little adjustment but would not by any means be an impossibility.' He paused by the door and stared down at her. 'However, for the time being at least, that is not on the agenda. My work takes me all over the world but I am primarily based in London.'

Julia breathed a sigh of relief. For all the changes that Nicola's presence in her life entailed, she would be lost without her. They had always been close, more so now. She uneasily wondered whether Nicola didn't serve the even greater purpose of filling the void in her life, the same void she denied having to her mother whenever the question was raised.

'So I shall see you on Saturday?' she said shakily and he nodded.

'About ten-thirty?' He pulled open the door but instead of walking to his car leaned indolently against the door frame and stared down at her. 'And don't forget.'

'Forget what?'

'Why, Julia, that we're lovers, of course.' His dark eyes roamed over her flustered face, a sensation he enjoyed thoroughly, then he succumbed to the wicked urge that had been plaguing him all night and he lowered his head, covering her startled mouth with his. It was a fleeting kiss, a shadow of a caress, and it tasted as sweet as honey.

And as paralysing as an electric shock, Julia thought numbly as he straightened and turned away as though nothing had happened.

And she had worried about the dangers of him trying to remove Nicola, to take her to Italy to live!

What about the danger lying far closer on her doorstep? She brushed her mouth with the back of her hand but she was still trembling by the time she made it to bed.

CHAPTER FOUR

'I AM beginning to have a whole new outlook on the word *exhaustion*,' Riccardo said to her on the Saturday afternoon as the three of them made their way back to the house.

Julia looked over Nicola's head in the taxi and caught his eye. 'Perhaps it was a mistake to promise that she could choose whatever toy she wanted.' But she couldn't make a big deal of it. It had not been a case of buying his daughter's affections, more trying to win them using the only currency with which he was familiar, namely money. Moreover, she was grateful that in his daughter's presence, he had been the epitome of charm and politeness, with none of those searing looks that were aimed to remind her of her criminal status in his eyes.

She was also grateful that there had been no mention of that farewell kiss of a couple of evenings before, and in fact, she had reached the point of wondering whether she might have dreamt the whole thing.

'I didn't realise that women began procrastinating from as young an age as five,' he responded drily, raising his eyebrows in bemusement.

'Are you talking about me?' Nicola asked, perking up at the mention of her age, and he smiled down at her, tempted to cradle the back of her dark head with his hand. He was aware of Julia looking at him and had to force himself not to look up suddenly and catch the expression on her face.

'We're wondering how come it took you three hours to finally choose your marker set and a handbag,' Julia said, smiling. 'They were the first things you saw!'

'I know, but I wasn't sure… I'm going to draw a picture of Mum and Martin,' Nicola said earnestly, then she turned to Riccardo. 'Would you like me to give it to you?'

Dark eyes clashed with grey ones.

'Of course. That would be very nice,' he said, only the tiny muscle beating in his jaw a sign of his thoughts. Strange, he had been gradually lulled into a sense of family, of belonging, and had almost forgotten that he was still on the outside looking for a way in. He averted his face and stared out of the window, watching the crowded streets race by.

'And maybe you could also draw a picture of a house,' Julia intervened hastily; 'you know how brilliant you are at drawing houses. A lovely tall house like the one you live in, with a red roof and a blue door.'

'Our door isn't blue.'

'Well, cream, then.'

'Will Gran be there when we get back? I want to show her what I got.'

'No, no, I don't think she will be. We can go visit tomorrow.'

'Will you be coming over tomorrow?' Nicola addressed her father and he turned round to look at her. The long, dark hair fell in a tumble along the little shoulders, rippling down her dark green anorak with the patches on the elbows. Her legs stuck out along the seat of the chair, not long enough to dangle over the edge, and her feet were encased in sturdy trainers that, she had proudly pointed out to Riccardo, lit up every time she walked.

He didn't even know whether he could answer that question without first getting permission from her aunt. He knew that it was irrational to continue feeling angry when anger did nothing to alter reality, but he could still feel it take him over.

What did Julia know of loss? he wondered. Loss like he felt whenever, it seemed, he rested his eyes on his daughter. Nothing.

Why shouldn't he make her find out? He had felt the way her mouth had trembled under his and he knew that under the self-control lay passion. He could stoke that passion and then when he walked away from her she too could feel some of the pain he was enduring now. Never as much, but enough.

He raised his eyes slowly to Julia's and held her stare.

'Why don't we play it by ear, Nicky, OK?' Julia said eventually.

'Does that mean yes or no?'

'It means we're not too sure yet,' Riccardo said gently, 'although I would love to come visit tomorrow. Maybe take you to the zoo, check and see how those animals are doing in this cold weather.'

This time when Julia looked at him it was with a frown of disapproval and Riccardo met her eyes with an edge of steel, while between them Nicola began bristling with excitement at yet another weekend treat in store. Not even Julia's dampening suggestion that they might be busy in the morning was enough to deter her enthusiasm.

'You shouldn't have made a promise like that,' was the very first thing Julia said once the taxi had dropped them off at the house, but she had to keep her voice low so that their conversation was not overheard.

'But I have nothing planned for tomorrow.' Riccardo feigned innocence. 'So why not? Did you not think that today was a roaring success?'

Julia didn't answer. She turned the key to the door and was instantly greeted by her mother, face aglow with excitement to find out how their day had gone.

Julia groaned inwardly.

'You didn't tell me you were coming over, Mum,' she said as brightly as she could, harking back with a sense of foreboding to their most recent conversation, during which her mother's seemingly incessant preoccupation with her daughter's man-less state had taken an alarming twist.

'I mean, Jules,' her mother had said coyly, 'he is very good looking, isn't he? And I must say, I've warmed to him since I've seen how he is with Nicola. Not a man to shirk his responsibilities like so many young people today.'

'Where are you going with this, Mum?' Julia had asked, as though she couldn't see very well for herself exactly where it was leading.

'It's not going anywhere.' But there had been no time to release any sighs of heartfelt relief. 'I'm just saying that you don't seem to have met any nice young men yet and why not seize the opportunity to get to know him? You're bound to naturally find yourselves getting close because of Nicola.'

Julia had wanted to point out that Riccardo Fabbrini was about as nice as a roving python on the lookout for its next meal, but she had resisted. Her mother was gradually succumbing to Riccardo's well-directed charm and Julia felt powerless against it.

'Oh, I decided I'd drop by on the spur of the moment, darling. Hope you don't mind that I let myself in.' Her mother's voice brought Julia back from her thoughts and she glanced a little anxiously around at Riccardo, who was listening to their conversation with his head tilted to one side, for all the world as though he could hear every thought running through her head.

'Perhaps you could take Nicky into the kitchen and get her something to drink, Mum,' Julia said with another bright smile. 'I just want to have a quick word with... Mr...um...'

She waited, tense as a coiled spring, until her mother and Nicola had vanished safely out of sight, then spun around to face him, her cheeks ablaze with colour.

'Look…um…'

Riccardo watched her in unhelpful silence. Not so much as a word of encouragement passed his lips as she wiped her hand feverishly across her brow.

'I had to tell Mum about…um…this idea of yours that you and I should appear to be…'

'Lovers?' he supplied, plucking the least helpful expression he could think of and folding his arms.

'Going out!' Julia corrected through gritted teeth. 'I had to just in case Nicky mentioned anything.' She paused and waited for him to fill the ensuing silence, which he didn't. 'It's just a bit of an awkward situation at the moment…um…because Mum's got it into her head that it's a splendid idea. In fact, if she seems to behave as though we really *are* going out instead of just pretending because of the situation, I want you to just ignore her.'

'I'm afraid you've lost me.'

I wish I could, Julia thought desperately. By connecting Riccardo with his daughter she had never envisaged that her own life would be so heavily involved. She was aware of him whenever he was around and had found herself thinking of him whenever he wasn't. When he came too close to her she had the urge to run.

'In words of one syllable, Mr Fabbrini…'

'Riccardo. Try not to forget.'

Julia ignored him. 'Mum might just lay on the encouragement a bit thick, but don't take any notice of her. She's just a little worried about me and she's got it into her head…'

'Worried about you?'

'Worried about me being single and having Nicola under

my care,' Julia snapped. 'She's decided that my life would be a lot better if I had a man around to help and for some strange reason she thinks that you...that you...'

'Might fit the bill?' He raised his dark eyebrows expressively and watched her squirm in embarrassment. It seemed, he thought, that fate was smiling on him.

'Course, she couldn't be more misguided if she tried,' Julia was telling him firmly. 'You're the last person in the world I would look at twice and I know you feel the same about me.'

'How do you know that?'

'The little brown sparrow?' She reminded him of his throwaway remark.

'Were you insulted by that?' he murmured softly and his eyes flicked over her so that she could have kicked herself for mentioning it in the first place. With men like Riccardo Fabbrini, arrogant to the point of distraction, it did not pay to look as though you gave the slightest bit of attention to anything they said.

'I was indifferent to it,' she lied bravely. 'I was merely using your expression as an example of how you felt about me and how I feel about you. Anyway, that's the situation as it stands. And by the way, please don't go arranging anything with Nicola that includes me without consulting me first.' She had added that last bit as a means of regaining some kind of control and she saw his mouth tighten, although he gave her a curt nod by way of concession.

His resolve hardened as he followed her into the kitchen. *Ask permission to arrange anything with his own daughter!* He felt a kick at the thought of wrapping her around his little finger. In fact, he doubted that he had felt such a kick before in his life. Women had come to him. The idea of active pursuit was intoxicating.

Nicola and Jeannette were in the kitchen, chatting animatedly about what they had done. Julia realised that she had not seen her niece so excited for a while. Her markers were already out of their pack and the handbag, a silver sparkly thing with a picture of Tigger embroidered on the front, was open, ready to be filled.

Julia's breath caught in her throat. When was she going to tell her about Riccardo? When would the time be right? She herself might find him arrogant and egotistic but Nicola didn't. Nicola enjoyed the attention he lavished on her. She enjoyed the way he listened to what she said without interrupting, as though every childish word that crossed her lips was of immense importance. It wouldn't be long before he would ask to take his daughter out without the irritating presence of a chaperon, and then he would take her completely. Take her to meet his family in Italy for a holiday, then he would move in for full custody.

'And we might be going to the zoo tomorrow!' Nicola was announcing, her eyes sliding across to Julia to see whether this comment could be slipped past without contradiction.

'Actually,' Jeannette said casually, fussing with the markers, 'I thought you two might like a bit of time of your own. In fact, that was one reason that I thought to come over. I could stay here and babysit Nicola so that you could both go out somewhere, for a meal perhaps.' She looked at Riccardo. 'Julia hasn't had much of an opportunity to go out recently...'

Julia felt a rush of humiliation and anger. She could feel the colour invade her face but she pinned the brightest smile to her lips because Nicola was looking at her.

'It's been a long day, Mum. We're all tired.'

'Nonsense.' Riccardo's voice cut short her litany of excuses and Julia looked at him in veiled surprise. He stepped forward, dominating the kitchen with his sheer size and overwhelming presence. He wasn't looking at her, though. He was looking at her mother and his mouth was curved into a smile of satisfaction. 'What a good idea! I know an excellent nightclub. Very good food and a very good band. After a long day shopping I think we could both do with a bit of relaxation, don't you, *Julia*?' He faced her with a smile and Julia wondered whether it was only she who could read the threat behind it. But why on earth would he *want* to go out with her, when there was no need?

'I—I...' she stammered desperately.

'It's not as though you need to get up early in the morning,' Riccardo continued, pinning her into a corner from which retreat was virtually impossible. 'Unless, of course, you intend to work on a Sunday...'

Jeannette watched these proceedings with delight. If she had harboured any doubts about him it was plain to see that she now genuinely liked him. How had he managed to do that?

'Gran and I will have fun here, Aunty Jules,' Nicola said.

'I'll go home and change quickly,' Riccardo said, moving towards her, 'and I'll be back to pick you up at seven-thirty.' He added in a low voice, 'I hope you'll be ready when I come.' He turned to face her, his broad back towards Jeannette and Nicola, blocking them out. 'And if you're not I shall come to your bedroom and fetch you, whatever your state of dress, so don't think about getting a sudden headache.'

'I refuse to be manipulated!' Julia said feebly, which only served to feed his anger at his own impotent frustration at *her* hands. Every minute spent in the company of his daughter was making him realise just how much he had missed and the slight brunette in front of him was part of the reason he had missed out. No good her denying it. If she had wanted she could have persuaded her brother to take a stand for what was right, persuaded Caroline to let him know about the pregnancy. Caroline had never been able to sustain an argument. She would have listened to reason, would have listened to someone as outspoken and forceful as Julia. For him to hear her talk about being manipulated almost made him laugh.

She would soon discover the nature of manipulation.

'I'll see you at seven-thirty.' With that, he turned to say goodbye to Jeannette, resisting the urge to kiss Nicola, and then stalked out of the kitchen.

He could feel excitement pulsing through his veins as he fired the engine of his car and drove back to his apartment. It took him a mere thirty-five minutes to make it there, using the back-roads of London which were fairly free of traffic. As he showered and changed he looked around his penthouse flat and pictured her there. He imagined her timidly entering, timid because she was not the sort of girl who slept around, who allowed herself to be taken to a man's apartment unless she had spent months building up a friendship first.

But however timid she might be, however cautious, she wouldn't be able to help herself. She would be in the grip of the same urgent need to make love as he would be. She would be excited, apprehensive, shaking with the anticipation of being taken by him.

He towelled himself dry and shaved quickly, with the towel wrapped around his waist. As he shaved he allowed his imagination to roam. To picture how her pale skin would look against the black leather of the sofa in his living room. He slowly stripped her of her sensible clothing, her weekend uniform of jeans and baggy jumpers, he removed her spectacles so that he could see the dark flecks in her grey eyes. He imagined her in tousled, panting disarray on his bed, tangled amid his bedclothes, tangled with *him*, limbs entwining with limbs, hands roving to touch and feel and explore.

She would beg him to bring her to a shuddering orgasm and would blush furiously as she pleaded for satisfaction.

He found that he had to drive at a more leisurely rate back to her house, in order to let his own excitement subside.

Her face was stiff with apprehension and exasperation at being wheedled into a date when she pulled open the front door to him.

'I don't see the point,' she grumbled as she slid into the passenger seat and primly gathered her pale grey flared skirt around her.

'The point of going to a nightclub?' Riccardo enquired, shooting out of the drive and expertly manoeuvring the car along the dark lanes away from her house. 'Or the point of going to a nightclub with *me*?'

'There was absolutely no need to jump at Mum's suggestion.'

'But you hardly ever get out,' he drawled lazily. 'I thought I would be doing you a favour. You know what they say about all work and no play...'

Julia glared ineffectively at his averted profile. She had no idea where they were going, but she suspected that she would not be dressed correctly for the venue. Her grey skirt was smart but hardly the height of fashion, and her strappy silk vest was covered by a dark grey jacket which she had no intention of removing. It left too much of her thin body exposed for her own comfort.

Riccardo, on the other hand, looked as magnificent as she suspected he would. His crisp white shirt emphasised the burnished gold of his skin and his suit, charcoal-grey, was impeccably and she suspected, lovingly hand-tailored.

From where she was sitting, she could smell the clean masculine scent of his aftershave.

'Relax,' he said into the silence. 'You're here now, why not enjoy it?'

'Where are we going?'

'Oh, just a little club I know. Very small. Not very fancy at all, so there's no need for you to feel self-conscious.'

'I don't feel self-conscious,' Julia threw at him, huddling in her unfamiliar outfit and feeling like a badly dressed teenager on her way to a prom night.

'Yes, you do. I can feel it.' He reached out with one hand and curled his long fingers along the back of her neck, gently massaging. Julia gave a squeak of alarm and drew away as much as she could. 'The tension is in your shoulders.' His fingers slipped a little lower, dipping under the collar of her jacket to knead her collar-bone, and just when she was about to tell him to *stop touching her immediately*, he took his hand away and replaced it on the steering wheel.

Julia could feel her heart hammering like a steam engine inside her. His cool fingers against her skin had sent a rush of fire through her, igniting her sensitive breasts and making her body ache.

'So tell me, why is your mother so desperate to have you married off?' Riccardo asked, his voice steady, composed and mildly interested.

'Aren't all mothers desperate to see their children married off?' Julia had to work very hard at keeping her voice as steady as his, but she was uncomfortably aware that her body was still in a state of heady response to his passing touch.

'That may very well be so,' Riccardo agreed. 'I know my *mama* was overjoyed when Caroline and I married. True, she wasn't Italian, but she could overlook that because I had spent so much of my time in England that it was almost natural for me to marry an English girl, and what an English rose Caroline was.'

'She must have been very disappointed when things... didn't work out,' Julia said as she found herself drawn into the conversation against her will.

'Disappointed but not, she afterwards informed me, hugely surprised.'

'Why not?'

'She told me that she worried that Caroline was not fiery enough for me but she had said nothing at the time because she had the notion that opposites might attract and that Caroline's lack of spirit might be just what I needed.'

Riccardo had never confided these personal details to anyone before. He was not a man who shared confidences or even allowed people to know how he felt about matters he deemed private. It felt right, however, to be talking to Julia about it and he decided, with the cool-headed logic which had been his byword for as long as he could remember, that he was simply getting her to relax by throwing her titbits of his personal life. Stirring her interest so that she would no longer see him as a threat. As long as she saw him as her enemy, someone to be distrusted, she would not respond to him and he was aggressively and thrillingly determined to win her response.

'Opposites do often attract,' Julia agreed slowly.

'Or else they repel. In our case, the latter.' He swung his car into a small forecourt jammed with expensive-looking cars, and when Julia looked at the clock on the dashboard she realised with a start that they had been driving for longer than she expected. Driving right out of London from the looks of it, because the street was broader and far less congested with houses and buildings than the streets in central London.

The nightclub itself was brightly illuminated on the outside and resembled someone's house, albeit a commanding, ivy-clad red-bricked house with a doorman incongruously standing to attention outside.

It took several minutes to locate a parking space, and Julia felt another rush of nerves as they walked towards the club, clutching her jacket around her with her little bag hanging from one hand.

The sudden pressure of his hand on the crook of her elbow was surprisingly comforting. As was the ease and assurance with which he led them inside, his hand still cupping her elbow. The room, staggered on two levels with a galleried landing forming a semicircle around the ground floor, was crowded, with people on the dance floor swaying about to the strains of slow jazz music. Waitresses buzzed between tables, carrying enormous trays above their shoulders on the flat of their hands and paying not the slightest bit of attention to the band performing on the podium.

They worked here and were familiar with the atmosphere. Julia, though, was not. As a teenager she had been to one or two nightclubs, noisy, dark places with too many people, no seating to speak of and beer being spilled over shoes and clothes. But this was a new experience for her.

She looked bewildered, Riccardo thought, his dark eyes taking in her open mouth. He felt an irrational swell of pleasure at being the one to introduce her to an experience she had obviously never had before. And she lived in London! What had she done with herself for all her adult life? She was no longer even aware of his hand on her and he took the opportunity to circle her waist with his arm, guiding her towards the table to which the waitress was leading them.

'I take it you have not been to this nightclub before,' he said, swinging his chair closer to hers so that they could speak comfortably above the music. His arm brushed against hers.

'I haven't been to any nightclub for years,' Julia confessed, turning to look at him, taken aback because he was so close to her.

'Not something that responsible teachers do?'

'Are you saying that one has to be irresponsible to come to a place like this?' She hadn't noticed that he had given the waitress an order for drinks but he must have because the young, leggy girl in her small black dress approached them now with a silver bucket in which rested a bottle of chilled white wine, and she expertly placed two wine goblets in front of them and, on a nod from Riccardo, poured them each a glass. Julia dived on hers with the abandon of someone suffering from fluid deprivation.

He laughed and his eyes dipped to the peach-smooth skin visible beneath her cropped jacket. He would be eating that peach later, he resolved, and conquest would taste as sweet as nectar.

'I would not dream of bringing a responsible woman like yourself to a den of iniquity. As a matter of fact, this is a very popular haunt with businessmen entertaining clients. It is more exciting than a restaurant and there is more scope for deals to be discussed than in the bowels of a theatre or an opera house.' Her eyes behind the spectacles were tentative and interested. She was putting aside her natural wariness of him and that in itself gave him a spurt of pleasure. Her face was soft, her mouth parted on a question.

'You come here often, I take it.'

'I have been here several times.' He removed his jacket, transferring his small black leather wallet to his trouser pocket. 'It's a good place to de-stress.'

Julia took another sip of her wine, her eyes drifting to his fingers loosely entwined on the table top. Riccardo, from above the rim of his wine glass tilted to his lips, saw everything, even noticed her slight tremor as she gathered herself and began to stare at the jazz band instead of his hands. Hands that were itching to touch her, and he wryly admitted to himself that evening the score was only part of the deal.

'Where do you go when you want to wind down?' he prompted, placing his glass on the table and circling the rim with one long finger. 'Has Nicola severely curtailed your social life?'

Julia shrugged.

'What does that gesture mean?' He mimicked her shrug. 'That she has or that she hasn't?'

'It's a little harder going out now in the evenings than it used to be. It means I have to make arrangements with Mum in advance. But don't think for a minute that I find it a hardship. I've always adored my niece and she's a joy to have around, even though it's a joy gained through circumstances I would never have wished and could never have foreseen.' Her eyes slipped to his finger trailing the glass and she hurriedly looked away, drowning her confusion by gulping down the remainder of her wine, only to find her glass refilled instantly.

'And where do you go when you make these arrangements?' he asked softly.

'Cinema. Wine bar. Sometimes to the theatre with friends, although on a teacher's salary I've always had to watch where my money went.'

'And now?'

Julia frowned. 'And now what?'

'Do you still have to watch your money? Or did my ex-wife and her husband make sure that you were provided for?' When she had first come to him he had instantly assumed that money must be at the root of her searching him out. Now he realised that she belonged to one of those rare species of women who were not impressed by how much money he had. He sat back in his chair and proceeded to look at her with a closed expression, trying to work her out.

'All of the money from the sale of your house went immediately into a trust fund for Nicola,' she replied coolly, 'and I was left enough to make sure that she doesn't seriously want for anything. So you can rest assured that I won't be knocking on your door, asking for handouts.'

'But it wouldn't be considered a handout, would it?' he told her in a hard voice. 'I've been willing to go along with your game plan, putting my feelings on hold *for the moment*, but I intend to assume full financial responsibility for my child.'

Julia had known that this would arise. In fact, she was surprised that it hadn't arisen sooner. She had a glimpse of a man biding his time and she shivered at the thought of it.

'I understand,' she began quietly, 'but I think you ought to concentrate on the most important thing, which is building a strong relationship with her so that it will be almost natural for her to accept you as her father when the time comes...'

'Don't preach to me on what I should and shouldn't do.' He leaned forward and placed his hands squarely on the table. 'For the moment, I am content to bring presents and then fade obligingly into the background, but rest assured that within the next few weeks I shall want you to produce a complete breakdown of Nicola's expenses, including a financial statement of the money that has been put in trust for her.'

'Because money is so important, isn't it?' Julia said tightly, gripping the stem of her wine glass.

Riccardo sighed heavily. 'It is simply a factor that I intend to take into consideration. Now, instead of sitting here and pointlessly sniping at one another, why don't we go and dance? Enjoy the evening.' He read the hesitation on her face and wanted to yank her out of her indecision by pulling her to the dance floor, but he waited in silence for her answer.

What was it about this woman? he wondered. One minute he was intrigued by her, intrigued enough to almost forget the part she had played in the situation that now existed. The next minute she was firing him up in a way he could recall no one doing in his life before, not even during his long climb to towering success, during which he had had to wage war with his adversaries and establish boundaries beyond which no one would be permitted to cross.

Even in his personal life, the women he had gone out with had respected his boundaries, had known their limits and had never crossed them. This woman boldly ignored every boundary he had laid down without raising her voice and then sat back and watched him rage in stubborn silence.

Dammit, did he want to seduce her to even a score or did he want to seduce her to prove to himself that he was still a man who could control his life, private and public?

'I'm not a brilliant dancer,' Julia was forced to admit awkwardly. And she would probably be even less adequate with this man's arms around her. Just the thought of it was enough to make her feel sick.

'Nor am I.'

'I don't believe you.'

'Then why don't I prove it to you? We can step on one another's feet and decide who is the worse.' He held out his hand and Julia reluctantly slipped her hand into his, feeling his fingers link through hers with a sudden, blinding panic.

'And you have to take your jacket off,' he murmured.

Julia blushed furiously, but obeyed, slipping the short jacket off her shoulders and then instantly feeling exposed in her small, silky top with the spaghetti straps.

She had hardly been listening to the band and was now aware that they were playing a slow number. It seemed that the atmosphere in the club aimed to be mellow, and as such the musicians complied, playing a selection of sexy, down-beat tunes, most of which were vaguely recognisable.

He led her onto the dance floor, which was darkly intimate and pulled her into his arms. His head lowered so that she could feel his mouth brushing her hair and her breasts pushed against his broad, hard chest.

He had been lying, as she had known he was, about his dancing. He was a superb dancer, his movements easy and fluid, and her body gradually picked up the sway of his, moving in time to his rhythm. As they danced he gently ran his finger along her exposed back and it was all Julia could do to keep her feet steady.

'See. I told you I was an abysmal dancer,' he laughed softly into her ear and for one terrifying moment she wished that she could feel his tongue flick there, then move to her lips, explore the soft insides of her mouth, which were trembling in a combination of horror and, she had to admit the truth, sheer, overwhelming craving.

CHAPTER FIVE

RICCARDO, feeling that small shiver of awareness, pressed home his advantage. He coiled his fingers through her hair, enjoying the sensation of it falling silkily over his hand. Most if not all of the women he had dated in the past had been staggeringly beautiful, sophisticated creatures with perfectly styled hair, hair that was secured in place with expensive lotions and hairsprays and was not destined to be threaded through a man's fingers.

Everything about this woman, however, was completely natural. Her thick shoulder-length hair felt smooth and clean. Her perfectly oval face was virtually free of make-up, aside from a pale shade of lipstick and a hint of blusher.

He pulled her fractionally closer to him so that she could feel his body against hers. He wanted her to read the signals he was giving her. He wished, in fact, that he could crawl inside her head and have a bull's-eye view of what was going on in her mind. But he would move slowly. Any direct moves would send her running in the opposite direction.

'Whoever told you that you weren't a good dancer was lying,' he murmured and, just for the sheer hell of it and because he wanted to see how she would react, he nibbled the tender flesh of her ear lobe. 'Now, how hungry are you? The fish here is excellent and not too heavy. We can keep dancing or we can have something to eat and then carry on.'

Had he just done what she thought he had? Had he actually caressed her ear? Julia realised that her feverish imagination was now making her actively hallucinate and she gratefully clutched the lifebelt he had thrown her, nodding vigorously in favour of the food option. In fact, she *was* hungry. Or, at least, she had been when she left the house.

They retired to their table and whilst they waited for their food to arrive Riccardo chatted pleasantly enough about anything and everything under the sun. Anything and everything that had nothing to do with Nicola. Talking about Nicola revived all his old anger at how he had been treated, kept in ignorance of her existence, and with the anger came the inevitable tension. Riccardo didn't want tension. Not right now. He had other plans in mind.

So he laughed and chatted and asked her questions about herself, whilst plying her with drink.

For the first time, the issue that lay between them like a yawning chasm faded into the background as Julia relaxed and told him about her childhood, omitting all mention of Martin. Slightly tipsy she might be, but she was aware of the temporary truce he had declared and she was willing to go along with it because he had been right. She had not gone out and enjoyed herself for quite a while, and it had been over a year since she had gone out on a date with a man. Kind, thoughtful Tim, who had turned from lover to friend to acquaintance all in the space of a short six months. It seemed to be her track record. No wonder her poor mother thought she would never settle down. No wonder, in her most private moments, she herself had her doubts.

'You're not drinking,' she accused when their main course had been cleared away and she had ordered a cappuccino in the hopes that it might sober her up a bit.

'I'm driving, remember? The two don't mix.'

'And I'm talking all about myself. You haven't told me anything about you.' *Talking about herself?* She had been positively garrulous, she thought wryly. What was it they said about alcohol loosening tongues? And with Riccardo, of all people! She had probably been boring him stiff, with her anecdotes about family life and school, but he had been too polite to divert the flow of conversation.

She waited until her coffee arrived and then drank it very quickly.

'What would you like to know?' he asked, watching her flushed face and the way she had the quirky habit of shoving her hair behind her ears when she felt nervous.

'What have you been doing since…is there anyone in your life? I never even thought to ask when I came to see you.'

'Is there anyone in my life…?' Riccardo drawled, sitting back and loosely linking his fingers on his lap. 'Right now I can say with my hand on my heart, that the only female in my life is Nicola. And yourself, of course.'

Yes, and for all the wrong reasons, Julia thought. She felt a puzzling sting of pain.

'You never thought about…getting married again?'

'You have obviously never been through a divorce. Believe me when I tell you that it is one of the most powerful reasons for doubting the institution of marriage. I learned to my cost that the state of wedded bliss can turn two people into strangers and from strangers into hostile opponents.' He laughed mirthlessly. 'Not that I would want to put you off.'

'It *can* be bliss for some,' Julia pointed out. 'My parents were very happily married.'

'As were mine. I guess you just have to say that it's a game of hit or miss, wouldn't you agree? But then again, what relationship isn't hit or miss?' He toyed with his coffee-cup and then took a sip. She had talked to him about her childhood, about what it was like being a teacher, about some of the plays she had seen, the restaurants she had been to, but she had said nothing about the men in her life, and Riccardo suddenly had a burning curiosity to find out about that private side of her. She was as contained as all his previous lovers had been obligingly informative. She retreated with the same speed as they had advanced.

'Shall we dance?' he asked lazily, upturning his hand and waiting for her to accept the invitation.

The dance floor was slightly less crowded than it had been, although the level of noise was higher, a muted but background surge of voices and laughter as the alcohol consumption increased and inhibitions diminished.

The tune carried a more upbeat tempo, and Riccardo swung her towards him, his long legs carrying the tune, his hips grinding gently against her body, his arms circling her back giving her no room to establish any space between them.

Julia felt heady and recklessly alive. It was warm in the room and a fine film of perspiration made her skin tingle.

'So tell me about your love life,' he whispered. 'Do teachers have love lives? I never used to think so at school until I was fourteen and had the pleasure of being in a class with a very voluptuous science teacher. I never realised how fascinating physics could be.' He laughed softly at the memory and Julia's lips curved into a smile.

'I can't imagine you taking apples in for your teacher,' she said.

'Perhaps not the apples but some highly charged fantasies. Until I discovered that she had a husband and a child, at which point I was cured of my adolescent infatuation and started concentrating my charged fantasies on slightly more attainable goals.' His mouth brushed the vulnerable curve of her neck. Any ideas about seduction to even a score had disappeared. He had wanted to taste that soft skin, had just not been able to resist.

Julia's breath caught in her throat. No, she most certainly had not imagined that. But she didn't want to stop him. He was turning her on and she wanted him to carry on turning her on. Three glasses of wine had put paid to her reservations.

'So does *this* teacher arouse fantasies in schoolboys?' he asked, his breath warm in her ear, tickling.

'Eight- and nine-year-old boys don't have fantasies,' she murmured, her face tilted so that her cheek pressed against the smooth cotton of his shirt. 'Or, at least, not of the nature you describe. I think their fantasies run more along the lines of joining the football team or acquiring a new computer game.'

'Shame. And what about your male teachers? Do they look slyly at you when you walk into the staff room? Do they entertain thoughts of stripping you naked and watching you come to them?' He was treading a very fine line here, he knew. He had never dreamed of asking any of his past conquests whether men had fantasised about them. Their responses would have been tediously predictable. A coy laugh and the knowing look in their eyes that told him just how fanciable they knew themselves to be, just what they could do for *him*.

He enjoyed knowing that his risqué questions were probably throwing her into a tizzy of embarrassment and confusion. The lighting was too subdued for him to see whether she was blushing or not, but he would put money on it. He discovered, with a pleasant little jolt of surprise, that the thought was electrifying.

'I don't think so,' Julia laughed nervously, feeling out of her depth now with this turn in the conversation. 'We only have three male teachers. Two are over fifty and the third, from what I gather, enjoys going on wildlife tours more than he enjoys going out with women. We think he might well be gay.'

'Hmm. That's not very stimulating, is it?' He dipped his hand just slightly under her blouse so that his fingers brushed her spine. 'So where do you go to find men who don't enjoy wildlife tours and might not possibly be gay? Mm?'

'I don't have much time to go scouring the city of London for men,' Julia replied vaguely. Teachers were, at least at her school, a fairly sociable lot and her last boyfriend she had met through a friend. It was a subject she did not want to talk about because she knew that he would begin questioning her, and in so doing would discover her appalling lack of an exciting sex life. She had never felt the sizzle of instant attraction, preferring to cultivate a friendship before launching into the dubious waters of romance.

'It's very warm here, isn't it?' she said, desperately trying to find a way of diverting the course of the conversation, and she was relieved when he agreed with her instantly.

'So shall we go back to the table?'

'I have a better idea. Why don't we wander outside for a while? The gardens at the back are quite extensive, believe it or not. One of the advantages of not having a nightclub in the heart of the city. And I could use a bit of cool air.'

Julia hesitated, but in the end she followed him out of the club and round the side, where the thought of cooling off had occurred to a number of people. On the way, they had collected her jacket from where it had been discarded by the table and their waitress had obligingly placed a reserve sign on the table.

The cold air hit her face like a balm and she stood still for a minute, breathing it in with her eyes closed, unaware that he was watching her and the way her slightly old-fashioned outfit emphasised the slenderness of her body. She had a naturally boyish build but seemed refreshingly unaware of how many women would have given their right arm for it. Almost no curves, he thought. Or none that was immediately apparent, although the feel of her breasts on the dance floor, pushing against him, was evidence enough that she was all woman.

He led her past the small groups of people cooling down after the heat inside, and towards the back garden, which was landscaped cleverly to convert a modest-sized plot into the illusion of a small copse. The ground was laced with trees, some evergreen, some bare of leaves, with intriguing, winding paths running between them.

'Perhaps we should head back in,' Julia said nervously as the solitude of their situation hit her. In summer she had no doubt that this garden would be teeming with people relaxing outside with their drinks before returning to the music and food, but in early March most people did not fancy the prospect of dawdling outside.

The cold was already beginning to bite through her thin jacket, and she pulled it tighter around her.

'Cold?' he enquired. In the absence of light, he was just a big, shadowy figure.

'A little.'

'There is that age-old technique for warming up,' Riccardo murmured, stepping closer to her, and Julia blinked furiously behind her spectacles. He ran his hands up and down her arms and felt a rough, primitive urge sweep over him. In every way she had played with his life, turned it on its head, and in more ways than one she had played with his mind, turning his hard-edged dislike into unwilling curiosity, taking the revenge he had coolly plotted and changing it into a genuine quest to control a woman who remained infuriatingly out of reach.

She looked at him. 'I don't think Management would like it if we lit a fire out here.'

Riccardo grinned, his teeth a sudden flash of white in the shadows. 'You're right. They might complain. Besides, I have no matches, have you?' He could feel her shivering beneath his hands. 'Nor do we have sun and a magnifying glass.'

'You were a boy scout?'

'Hardly.' He laughed softly. 'I just read a lot of useful books when I was a kid. I fancied myself marooned on an island, having to survive.'

There was a brief silence, during which they looked at one another, a brief, charged silence, pregnant with the possibilities of the moment.

Then he lowered his head and his mouth met hers. He had not realised the depth of his hunger to taste her lips until he felt hers cool and yielding. Her hands remained clasped protectively around her body as she inclined upwards to him.

'I can't do this with…these on…' He removed her spectacles and Julia whimpered at the brief interlude. She no longer cared about keeping her distance. She was waiting, no, yearning for him to kiss her again, and this time, as his mouth sought and found hers, she returned the kiss, her tongue sliding against his, her lips parted to receive his searing, hungry caress.

He pulled her arms away from her body and, with his hands behind her buttocks, pushed her towards him, grinding her so closely against his body that she could feel his hard erection pressing against her.

A wild abandon coursed through her veins and she moaned as his teeth nipped the arched column of her neck.

Her breasts were aching with the need to be touched, and as if sensing this, Riccardo shoved his hands up the silky top until he felt their soft swell under the strapless lace bra. He felt like a man making love for the first time. Every movement was fuelled with desperate urgency. He didn't want to gently make love to her, he wanted to take her right here and right now and satiate the primal urge tearing him apart.

With one swift movement he dragged the strapless bra down so that he could massage the twin peaks of her breasts with their tight, protruding nipples. As he massaged them she groaned with pleasure and every groan urged him on.

'Touch me,' he commanded, circling her wrist with his hand and guiding it to where his throbbing manhood needed the cool touch of her fingers. He unzipped his trousers and as she gripped his stiffness through his silk boxer shorts she gave a little cry of desire.

'Feeling a little warmer now?' he asked, punctuating the warmth of his breath in her ear with the damp coolness of his tongue.

Julia was beyond answering. The gardens could have been designed, she thought wildly, for this type of activity. The trees were a natural barrier against prying eyes and the scattering of benches a welcome respite for unsteady legs. Riccardo led her to one of these benches, and when she had sat down he splayed apart her legs and positioned himself between them, then he lifted her vest. Her bra was still pulled down and her breasts spilled over the top of it, forming erotic points that reminded him of nothing more than ripe fruits. Ripe fruits ready for eating, which was what he intended to do.

With a stifled groan he buried his face against her breasts

and began sucking, and her hands, hesitant at first, curled into his dark hair while her body slid down the bench until she was arching back to enjoy the erotic sensuous pleasure he was giving her.

She had no idea how this had happened and she didn't care. She had no experience of this sort of raw, carnal lust and she was a willing student. In fact, more than willing—eager. With her head thrust back, she blindly cupped her other breast, offering it to his greedy mouth and she kept her hand there as he suckled, the tip of his tongue flicking erotically over her engorged nipple.

When he removed his feasting mouth she felt the cool air against her bare skin and she twisted in protest, but he was already rucking up her skirt, and Julia's eyes flew open in shock.

He raised his head and smiled wolfishly at her. 'When you say no, do you mean no? Or do you mean yes, please?'

Julia pulled up her bra and shoved down her top but her frantic efforts at rearranging herself stopped there. She looked at him, ready to explore the most intimate region of her body in a way no other man had, and was rocked by excitement.

'I don't think…' she panted breathlessly. 'We can't… I've never…'

'Never felt a man's mouth down here?' To demonstrate the place he meant, he pulled aside her briefs and cupped her with his hands, pressing down until she squirmed. 'And do you want to?'

'We should go back in…side…'

He didn't answer. Instead he bent his head closer to her, his nostrils flaring as he breathed in the musky, womanly scent of her, fragrantly enticing. A thought flickered through his head and was gone before it had time to register. The thought that what he was doing was somehow dangerous, except how could it be? He was in the driving seat and fired with the need to possess. For the first time with this woman, he was on ground with which he was familiar. He would have preferred to have been making love in his king-sized bed in his apartment, but this had a thrilling feel of the stolen moment. He felt like an adolescent and that in itself was so novel a feeling that he thought he should not wish it away.

'If you really want to go inside,' he said unsteadily, 'then, of course, we will.'

Julia twisted like someone in the grip of a fever, a movement he took as surrender, and he lightly skimmed his tongue along the crease of her womanhood, her gasping shudder making him give a grunt of exquisite satisfaction.

He intensified the pressure of his tongue, pushing it deeper within her and holding her firm as she bucked against his hands. It was every bit as erotic as he had imagined it would be. More. He could feel every thread of shock in her at what he was doing and, even more powerful, the need for him to continue. He moved his tongue up and down, sliding into her moistness and licking the tiny bud that had her convulsing with lust.

She curled her fingers into his hair and tugged, her hands pleading with him to stop because he was driving her crazy, but he didn't want to stop. He wanted to take her to the brink and then complete their lovemaking by thrusting into her, like a stallion, so that he could see her face when she reached the dizzy heights of her orgasm.

It took a while for the sound of voices to penetrate Julia's numb, giddy world. It was only when the woman giggled, a high-pitched sound that drifted through the trees and insinuated that another couple had obviously come out for precisely the same as she had been doing, that Julia jerked up and back into the world of the living.

She stared down in horror at Riccardo, barely able to vocalise, but he was already standing up, cursing under his breath.

Julia sprang to her feet and tidied herself with trembling hands.

She had no idea what to say. What was there that she could possibly say? She must have gone completely crazy. She couldn't bring herself to look at him and had turned to head back hurriedly into the club, when he stopped her.

'Don't think you can run inside and pretend that none of this happened,' he grated harshly, furious at their interruption. He had been as fired up as she had been and could already see that she was retreating. Dammit, he was not going to let her retreat on him!

The amorous couple had obviously heard their voices and vanished into another part of the garden, as eager as they had been for privacy. Julia felt sick. Sick with shame and mortification and utterly bewildered by her behaviour.

Riccardo held onto her arms, forcing her to look at him, to acknowledge what had just taken place. He had invaded every pore of her body and now he wanted her to admit it. 'You opened a door and you can't tell me that you can shut it now!'

'*I* opened a door!' Julia spluttered.

'OK, we *both* did.'

'Things got a little out of control. I…I must have had too much to drink…'

'And don't blame the drink! You were as aware of what was going on as I was! And you were enjoying every minute of it!'

Julia stared at him in helpless, frustrated silence. She could feel the cold air wrapping itself around her.

'I'm cold and it's time to leave,' she said unsteadily and after a few seconds he released her.

'Not before we sort this thing out.'

'There's nothing to sort out. I…I don't know how…how we happened to…'

'Stop shying away from the bald truth. How we happened to make love.' With every passing minute she was withdrawing from him, shutting him out, and he was not going to allow her to do that. He had come too far to admit defeat now and walk away. Riccardo Fabbrini never walked away from unfinished business, and this was unfinished business as far as he was concerned.

'We happened to do it because we wanted each other. Still do.'

'It was a moment of madness!' she denied heatedly.

'When is lust ever not a moment of madness?' He sighed and raked his fingers through his hair. The truth was that he was still on fire and the even more gut-wrenching truth of the matter was that he would continue to be on fire until he completed the task he had set for himself, killed off the curiosity to possess her that was driving him crazy. No woman had ever sent his senses rocketing into orbit as this complex creature trembling in front of him had. 'Have you never experienced a moment of madness?' he asked wryly.

'Never.'

'Then you haven't lived.' Their eyes met for the briefest of seconds.

'Maybe not in your eyes.' Her voice sounded high-pitched and defensive. If he couldn't hear the fear in it then she certainly could. Fear of the sweeping tide of physical attraction that had bowled her over the minute he had laid his hands on her. And the attraction hadn't begun tonight. It had been simmering under the surface from the very first moment she had seen him. She had just flatly refused to acknowledge it.

He was so wrong in every respect. He was everything

Caroline had bitterly described him to be. Cold, ruthless, arrogant, a man who got what he wanted whatever the costs and at whatever price. She should have recoiled in disgust at the feel of his hands on her back and the warm breath against her cheek as they had danced, but the opposite had happened and she could not make sense of it. And she should have fled from the touch of a man who had been her sister-in-law's ex-husband, but Caroline had never loved him. Her brief infatuation had been a bright flicker before fading away. There was no betrayal there, but still…

Her heart was still hammering in confusion as they re-entered the club and she preceded him to their table, not bothering to sit down.

'We're not leaving yet,' he informed her, pulling his chair out and sprawling on it, magnificently and gut-wrenchingly masculine, his body lazily indolent as he summoned across their waitress and ordered a refill of coffee for them both. 'So you might as well stop hovering like a startled rabbit and sit down.'

A little brown sparrow? A startled rabbit? Apt that he described her as prey, when she saw him as a predator.

Julia reluctantly perched on her chair and looked at him. 'I don't see the point of conducting a post-mortem on what happened,' she said quietly. 'It did, for reasons I can't fathom…'

'For reasons it *suits you not to fathom*,' Riccardo corrected harshly.

'You're not attracted to me, Riccardo; you made that perfectly clear the very first time I met you. Remember?' Julia sat back to allow her cup of coffee to be placed in front of her, along with the individual plunger, a jug of cream and a bowl of rough sugar cubes.

'And the feeling was mutual, if I recall,' he drawled mockingly. 'Let's just say that time alters everything.' He leaned across the table, invading her space, and she felt her pulses quicken in automatic response. 'If we hadn't been so rudely interrupted we both know where it would have ended.' He smiled wolfishly at her, cutting through her defences and silencing the denial rising to her lips. His eyes locked with hers, making her feel giddy. 'You wanted me in you as much as I wanted to be in you. You were desperate for our foreplay to go further, darling, and I was as desperate as you were. Let's just face the truth and deal with it.'

'But why?' Julia cried. Why what? It was inconceivable that Riccardo Fabbrini was attracted to her. Something else was going on here, under the surface. It was easy for her to see why she had succumbed to him in a moment of passion and, whether he liked to admit it or not, under the influence of alcohol which had lowered her natural reserve. He was devilishly good-looking. There could be very few women who would not respond to his suffocating sexual magnetism. She might hate herself for her temporary weakness, might argue that it defied all logic, but she could still understand her response.

But she possessed no such irresistible qualities of attraction. So why had he seduced her? Because it had all the hallmarks of a seduction.

She was staring at him, trying to find the right words to express what was going on in her head, when a voice cut through the thick silence. Julia sat back and found that her body was rigid with tension and she was breathing rapidly, like someone slowly being deprived of oxygen.

'Riccardo! I've been trying to call you for three weeks! Where have you been?'

Riccardo cursed silently to himself and looked at the platinum-blonde staring down at him with angry, hurt green eyes. There could not have been a worse moment for Helen

Scott to make her appearance. She was dressed, as always, in an outfit that revealed the maximum amount of body without being indecent. Tonight, the colour was red, a bright, eye-grabbing red in the shape of a dress of minuscule proportions, and black shoes that added a further four inches to her already considerable height.

She drew up one of the two free chairs, completely ignoring Julia's presence and fixed him with doleful, accusing eyes.

'I've been busy,' Riccardo told her coolly. 'Have I introduced my date for the evening? Julia, this is Helen. Helen's a model, if you hadn't already guessed.'

'A model and your girlfriend.'

'Ex-girlfriend.' He sighed impatiently, acutely aware that Julia was looking between the two of them and forming opinions. Opinions, for some reason, he did not want her to form. He had never been ashamed of the series of fabulously built, good-looking blonde women who had adorned his arm since his divorce. In fact, he knew that he was the envy of most red-blooded males whenever he went out with one of these women. But he was ashamed now. He could imagine her judgemental, clever brain ticking away, forming conclusions about the kind of relationships he conducted with women, meaningless relationships with women who had never challenged so much as a pore of him. The fact that such relationships had suited him as much as the women in question now sickened him.

Julia, sitting back and watching, felt her heart turn to lead. If she had needed reminding of why exactly a man like him could never be attracted to a woman like her then she had received a very timely reminder. She didn't think that she had ever seen a woman as exquisite as the one sitting next to her, or rather draping her body across the table next to her. Where Caroline had been stunningly pretty, this woman was strikingly beautiful. Every feature was chiselled to perfection, from the arched slant of her eyebrows to the small, perfectly shaped nose and the wide curve of her mouth.

'I've been trying to get in touch with you,' Helen said huskily, the threat of tears in her voice. 'I love you, Riccardo, and I thought you loved me.'

'This is neither the time nor the place…'

'Then where is?' The full mouth trembled. 'I just want to talk with you. In private. I know we can work things out, I know it. I can't sleep, Riccardo, I can't eat. All I can do is think of you, of *us*.'

'There *is* no us, Helen.' His voice was gentle but Julia detected the thread of irritation in it and shuddered inwardly.

'But there could be! If you'll just give us another chance.'

'It didn't work out,' he told her flatly, 'and, if you recall, I never made you any promises. In fact, I was at pains to warn you that I was not on the lookout for commitment.'

'But—'

'There are no *buts*, Helen. You need to move on. I've moved on.' His eyes involuntarily flickered across to Julia and Helen followed his gaze, registering the woman next to her for the first time since she had sat at their table.

'Her? You're going out with *her*?' Her voice wasn't hard with criticism or resentment. It was bewildered, and that struck Julia more forcibly than if she had been punched in the chest by someone in a jealous rage. 'But you can't be. Look at *me*. How could you choose *her* over *me*?'

'Leave this table immediately.' He did not raise his voice by so much as a decibel. He didn't have to. Its very softness was the equivalent of a whiplash, and Helen blanched vis-

GET FREE BOOKS and a FREE MYSTERY GIFT WHEN YOU PLAY THE...

SLOT MACHINE GAME!

Just scratch off the silver box with a coin. Then check below to see the gifts you get!

YES! I have scratched off the silver box. Please send me the two FREE books and mystery gift for which I qualify. I understand I am under no obligation to purchase any books, as explained on the back of this card. I am over 18 years of age.

P2HI

Mrs/Miss/Ms/Mr ______ Initials ______

BLOCK CAPITALS PLEASE

Surname ______

Address ______

______

Postcode ______

Worth TWO FREE BOOKS plus a BONUS Mystery Gift!

Worth TWO FREE BOOKS!

Worth ONE FREE BOOK!

TRY AGAIN!

Visit us online at www.millsandboon.co.uk

Offer valid in the U.K. only and is not available to current Reader Service subscribers to this series. Overseas and Eire please write for details. We reserve the right to refuse an application and applicants must be aged 18 years or over. Offer expires 31st December 2002. Terms and prices subject to change without notice. As a result of this application you may receive further offers from carefully selected companies. If you do not wish to share in this opportunity, please write to the Data Manager at the address shown overleaf. Only one application per household.

The Reader Service™ — Here's how it works:

Accepting the free books places you under no obligation to buy anything. You may keep the books and gift and return the despatch note marked 'cancel'. If we do not hear from you, about a month later we'll send you 4 brand new books and invoice you just £2.55* each. That's the complete price - there is no extra charge for postage and packing. You may cancel at any time, otherwise every month we'll send you 4 more books, which you may either purchase or return to us - the choice is yours.

*Terms and prices subject to change without notice.

NO STAMP NEEDED!

NO STAMP
NECESSARY
IF POSTED IN
THE U.K. OR N.I.

THE READER SERVICE™
FREE BOOK OFFER
FREEPOST CN81
CROYDON
CR9 3WZ

If offer card is missing write to: The Reader Service, PO Box 236, Croydon, CR9 3RU ibly. When she stood up she turned fully to Julia and spoke in a wavering voice.

'I don't believe Riccardo is going out with you,' she said with tears in her eyes. 'He's always dated good-looking blondes. We used to joke about it, about the way he was always attracted to the same type.' She gave a stifled sob and raised her hand to her mouth, as if pressing down the emotion. 'I don't understand.' She turned away and blindly made her way, head bent, weaving through the tables until she had disappeared towards the other side of the room.

'I apologise for that,' he said roughly. 'Helen and I broke up before I met you. She obviously thought I was joking when I told her it was over.'

Julia didn't say anything. She understood everything and it made her blood run cold.

'I just didn't understand how you could actually be attracted to a *little brown sparrow* like me.' Her voice was mocking. It was easy to use derision to conceal her hurt, her hurt and her anger at herself, because she knew that somewhere deep inside she had half hoped that he really had been attracted to her. 'Now I understand that you weren't.'

'You understand nothing!' he bit out savagely and she smiled, distancing herself from the powerful, potently masculine man leaning towards her, his black eyes burning with intent.

'Oh, no, that's where you're wrong, Riccardo. They say that men go for certain models and very rarely deviate from form. You go for good-looking blondes. Helen said as much herself.' An icy calm had replaced the rampant chaos in her mind. 'You would never in a month of Sundays be seriously attracted to a brown-haired, bespectacled teacher like me. But you were willing to seduce me, weren't you, Riccardo? Because what you wanted wasn't *me*. You wanted to pay me back for what I did, for disrupting your life, for exploding a bomb in your highly organised, perfectly fine-tuned existence. I was the messenger who brought the bad news, and they say we always want to shoot the messenger. That's it, isn't it, Riccardo Fabbrini? You were prepared to set aside your high standards in the opposite sex because it suited you to use your charm on me, to what…make me fall in love with you? So that you could then walk away and teach me a lesson? Was that it?'

She waited for him to at least deny it, hoped desperately that he would, but the hesitation that greeted her accusation was answer in itself, and Julia stood up abruptly, sick to the stomach.

She should have listened to the warning bells in her head, should have kept her distance. She knew better now.

CHAPTER SIX

JULIA could feel the sting of tears at the backs of her eyes as she sat, stony-faced, in the car, her jaw clenched, staring straight ahead. Tears of mortification and hurt.

Riccardo slammed the driver's door behind him but instead of starting the engine he turned to her, leaning against the door.

'Look at me.'

'Take me home, please. Or I shall have to get out of the car and order a taxi.'

'Don't be ridiculous. You would have to wait hours if you ordered a taxi. They're not exactly lining the streets outside.'

'I am *not* being ridiculous! I just want to go home.' Ridiculous, though, was how she felt. Ridiculous in her prim grey outfit, dusted down especially for the occasion, sad and ridiculous.

Riccardo's jaw clenched and he took a few deep breaths. 'I'm sorry about what happened in there. I had no idea Helen would be there or else, naturally, we would have gone somewhere else.'

'Oh, yes, I'm sure you're sorry,' Julia's head snapped round and she glared angrily at him. They had parked at a fair distance from the front of the nightclub, but there was still enough light to throw his handsome face into angled relief. How she could ever have believed, even in the remotest corner of her heart, that this dark, breathtakingly sexy man could ever have touched her body with desire made her shudder with humiliation. 'Sorry because I exposed you for what you are! A man who feels that he can dominate everything and everyone in his life, do exactly what he pleases without thought for anyone else. No wonder Caroline cringed from you!'

'Don't you dare bring my ex-wife into this equation! You've jumped to conclusions and arrived at your own twisted explanations because of your own insecurities.' He was guiltily aware that there was an element of truth in her accusations, but instead of calming him down that only served to stoke his anger further. The minute he had touched her he had been consumed by a need far greater than anything he had experienced before and now…now he realised that his need had been controlling him all along. He had tagged on a few handy reasons to justify his burning desire to touch her, but the brutal truth was that he was attracted to this woman, deeply attracted to the woman who had purposefully wrought havoc with his life. The fact that it made no sense had pushed him into dealing with the unfamiliar sensation of being out of control in the only way he knew how. By trying to take over the reins, by trying to control his inexplicable feelings.

'Don't you dare talk to me about my insecurities,' Julia bit out harshly. 'You don't know a damn thing about me or my insecurities! You pigeonholed me into the enemy from day one and you never bothered to try and understand me or what motivates me! You think you know me because you think you know everything!'

The car was alive with tension; it crackled around them and crawled along her skin and into her bones.

'And you haven't pigeonholed *me*?' He laughed, a dry, unpleasant sound. 'I am Caroline's nasty ex-husband—have you forgotten? I'm the bastard who drove her into the arms of another man. Did *you* ever stop to think that the beast my ex-wife described to you could have felt pain? I might have stopped loving her…maybe I never really did love her. The illusion of love can be powerful but betrayal hurts. Did you ever consider that? Oh, no, you just assumed that I was a bastard and so it was all right to deny me my own daughter because I couldn't possibly have any redeeming features.'

Julia went white as he plucked the unarticulated thoughts from her head and laid them out in front of her in merciless detail.

'You took one look at Helen and decided that she represented the only type of woman I could possibly look at twice. But, as I said, you're looking in the wrong direction for your conclusions. Instead of throwing it at me, try throwing it at yourself. The fact is, you measured yourself against her and found yourself wanting.'

'That's not true! Now drive me home immediately.'

'And cut short this revealing conversation? I think not.' It shocked him to realise that the only thing he wanted to do, really wanted to do, was to finish what had been started in the gardens of the nightclub an hour ago. She sat there, spitting rage at him, as if he had struck a match and tossed it at her, and he wanted to touch her. It made such little sense that he almost shook his head in bewilderment. But he wasn't going to let her squirm away from this. He wasn't going to allow her to throw her frank observations in his face and then turn her back on him before he had a chance to throw a few of his own back at her.

'You have hang-ups about how you look, and your mother probably doesn't help matters by rattling on about marriage and settling down. Underneath that controlled exterior you're burning up with your own insecurities, which is why you think that a man who could bed a woman like Helen would never choose to bed you.'

'Do you have to use such coarse language?'

'Sometimes I'm a coarse man. I don't go around ducking behind civilised phrases when a few blunt words would do much better instead. But do you know what I think?' He leaned forward, crowding her, and Julia felt her heart begin to accelerate. Even though her mind was shrieking disdain, her whole body was reacting to his proximity. Her breasts were hardening and her eyes were compulsively drifting to the narrow line of his sensuous mouth. God, she wanted to touch it, wanted it to devour her, every part of her. It made her sick to think about it.

'I don't care what you think.'

'But you'll listen anyway,' he ground out. 'I think coarse men like me turn you on. I'll bet my house that you've spent your life going out with namby-pamby sissies in touch with their feminine sides.' He made a derogatory sound under his breath and Julia inclined her body towards him, so that their faces were almost touching.

She was so mad that she had to keep her hands clenched on her lap or risk slapping that knowing smirk off his face.

'It may not occur to you that some women happen to like men who are sensitive and kind and considerate and thoughtful! Men who don't act as though the entire universe is their own private playground to do with as they want!'

'Some women, but not you.' He knew that she was itching to hit him. Quite honestly, he could understand why, but God, he wanted her to admit that she had been powerless against him when he had touched her. 'You don't want a man you can order about like one of your schoolchildren. You want a man who will take you, and when he's finished you'll want to beg for him to take you again. Me.'

Julia laughed but to her own ears it sounded brittle and unconvincing. 'You! You flatter yourself!'

'Do I?' he murmured, his eyes flicking to her full mouth.

Abruptly, the atmosphere in the car changed. Julia drew her breath in sharply, wanting to look away but unable to tear her eyes from his lazy inspection of her face. She felt mesmerised, like a rabbit caught in the headlights of a car. Her lips parted and he raised his hand to trace the contours of her mouth.

'Stop it, please, Riccardo,' she mumbled weakly, and he gave a low, sexy laugh.

'Sure. But only because I can think of better places for my finger to be.' He removed her spectacles and placed them on the walnut dashboard, almost expecting her to pull away from him and not knowing what he would do if she did that. He didn't trust himself to behave like a perfect gentleman.

'Do you want to know where I want my hand to be?' he asked softly, and Julia shook her head dumbly and muttered,

'No.'

'Then you'll stop me, will you?' He slipped his hand under her shirt and hooked his finger under her bra, tugging gently until her breast popped out, and without taking his eyes from her face, he stroked her nipple, feeling his own arousal surge as his finger grated over the tightened bud.

Riccardo buried his face against the side of her neck, nipping her skin until Julia thought she would pass out from the twin sensations of his mouth against her skin while his finger rubbed her sensitised nipple.

She wanted to drag herself away from this madness, but her brain seemed to be wrapped in cotton wool.

He was taking advantage of her, proving a point, proving to them both that the craving she felt for him was beyond control, but she was powerless to resist. As soon as he laid one finger on her, her body went up in flames, and her hunger for him fanned the flames until the only consuming thing in her head was having him.

She arched back with a shuddering sigh, and he bent to lick her stomach while his hand slipped beneath her skirt and he felt the soft flesh of her parted thighs.

She was certain that he would be able to hear the furious hammering of her heart as he nuzzled upwards until he found her nipple with his mouth and he began pulling on it, sucking her breast into his mouth as she caressed his dark, bent head. His exploring finger had now insinuated itself down under her briefs and began rubbing erotically into her, drawing her feminine moisture up to dampen the throbbing bud of her womanhood.

Twisting to her side, Julia groped until she found the zipper of his trousers and tugged it down, grappling with the button on the waistband and feeling a surge of satisfaction as he groaned and helped her in her efforts towards his rigid manhood.

As her hand clasped around it he groaned again, his breathing as uncontrolled as her own.

Had Riccardo been right? Had she only ever sought out the gentle, unassuming men because deep down she had felt that they were all she could aspire to? Unthreatening men who politely kissed her and fumbled with her body as though embarrassed at being in female terrain? Had she steered clear of aggressive, dominant males, men like Riccardo, although she had never actually met anyone quite like him, because of her own lack of self-esteem in how she looked? Surely not… Yet here she was, turned on and utterly incapable of turning herself off!

She only removed her hand to wriggle out of her underclothes, scarcely believing what she was doing, eager to resume her exploration of his body. With a little shove, she pushed his head away from where his mouth was fastened to her nipple, nipping it and licking, and with her free hand she shakily undid the buttons of his shirt and ran her hand over his taut stomach before she flicked her tongue over his flat brown nipples.

This couldn't be happening, yet it was. The windows were misty but she still felt her instinctive modesty kick in when he commanded her to sit on him.

'I can't! We're in a car park,' she gasped and he gave a low growl of amusement.

'So what? No one's around and God, I want you. Now!'

Julia wondered whether slightly built frames were fashioned for making love in small places. Or maybe her own frantic need was sufficient to expedite what he had demanded. Her skirt, twisted around her, barely hampered her lithe transference from her own seat to his and she felt the thrust of him in her with exquisite, searing pleasure. Every pore in her body was tingling for satisfaction and all modesty was thrown to the winds as he freed her of her jacket and ordered her to take off her camisole and bra for him so that he could see her as they made love.

She heard his sharp intake of breath as her breasts were exposed and felt a heady, dizzying wave of power as his eyes raked over her nakedness. She leant forward so that her breast dipped towards his mouth and slowly began to move on him, watching with heightened senses as his tongue flicked to capture her nipple in his eager mouth.

He slipped his hands around her waist and her movements quickened until they were soaring, beyond caring who might pass by and be curious at what was going on in the expensive Jaguar with the steamed-up windows.

Julia felt her shuddering peaks of excitement ebbing and rising once again, and then, drained, she fell against his broad chest, wanting nothing more than to snuggle into him and let her spent drowsiness take her away.

Riccardo stroked her hair. God, he had just had the most intense orgasm he could remember, and he could take her again. What the hell was this all about? He sighed, perplexed, and she straightened, her languid gaze focusing finally on his face.

'My God,' Julia whispered. She was suddenly aware of her state of undress and began to edge off him, but his big hands covered her hips, holding her firmly in place. He looked at her, then lowered his eyes to roam over her upper body. Her breasts were perfectly proportioned for her slight body, pert and upright, with big, rosy nipples. Just looking at them made Riccardo stir in automatic response. He reached out and inserted his finger under one, gently stroking, then he blew and watched her nipple tighten as it reacted to his breath.

'Riccardo, no.'

'You doubt that I could give a repeat performance?' he drawled, catching her eyes with his. 'Believe me, I could.'

She could believe him. Not only was he the epitome of virile man, but she could also feel him hardening inside her, filling her out. Julia could have stayed where she was, pleasuring herself in his rampant feasting of her body, but the niggling doubts that had been cast aside when passion took over were now making themselves felt.

They had just made love, but why was it, when she looked at him, that the last thing stamped on his face was love?

She slowly lifted herself from him and slipped back into her seat, reaching out for her spectacles, but instead of putting them on, she held them loosely on her lap.

'What is it?' he asked sharply, turning to her.

'Nothing.' Everything, she thought. She had just performed the most intimate act that could exist between a man and a woman but that was where the intimacy stopped.

He had seduced her with his tongue and with his body, but not because he loved her or even cared about her.

He had talked around her accusations, had tried to make her feel as though she had misjudged his intentions, but now, when Julia thought about it, she realised that he had not denied any of the things she had hurled at him. He had not denied his intent to seduce her as a payback.

She bent over and began putting on her top, all too aware of her vulnerability as she struggled into it, her breasts dancing and almost hurting as his eyes raked over them.

Then she gathered the rest of her garments, shamelessly thrown off in the heat of passion.

Riccardo watched and waited. For the first time in his life, he didn't know where this situation was leading. He knew where he wanted it to go. He also knew that to push his point would meet with a blank wall.

'We really should go, Riccardo,' Julia said.

'You're doing it again. Why don't you say what's on your mind instead of giving me your British reticence? We've just made love and—'

'It means nothing.' It hurt to say it, but she had to. She had given herself to a charmer, to someone whose intentions were questionable at the best and downright cruel at the worst. She had ignored her better instincts and had melted at his touch and she was not about to put herself in line for his eventual gloating.

'No, it means we gave in to a moment of curiosity...'

'A moment of curiosity?' Riccardo's voice was grimly cold and Julia flinched, but reminded herself of what she meant to him. She was the woman who had sided with the enemy and deprived him of his child, she was the mousy, brown-haired sparrow to whom, as he had casually informed her at their first meeting, he could never be attracted. Because he went for blondes. Blondes like

Caroline, like Helen, like heaven only knew how many other woman discarded somewhere along the way.

Blondes because maybe, for him, the only woman he had really ever loved had been blonde. Blonde, childlike Caroline, who had finally broken free of his invasive personality.

Julia felt a stab of jealousy and pain rip through her, leaving in its wake the shattering realisation that what she wanted from him was not just sex, but much more. Because what she felt for him was not simply physical attraction, but the dawning of an emotion that ran far deeper.

She steeled herself. 'Sure. You're a man of the world.' She shrugged and continued to stare blindly out of the window, not trusting herself to look in his direction. She had already discovered, to her cost, what he could do to her with just a glance. 'You know how powerful curiosity can be, and,' she continued lightly, 'you were curious about me. Angry as well, but curious too. Maybe because I am so different from the kind of women you're accustomed to dating.'

'And you?' he asked softly, giving nothing away. 'You seem to have explained my motives to yourself, so care to explain your motives to me? Or shall I follow your lead and just take a pot-shot?'

Julia would not succumb to arguing. He won every argument. He could twist her words into knots and leave her floundering.

'Me?' she mused, eyes still averted. 'I was curious too, believe it or not. You were right. All the men I've ever dated, not that there has been a long line of them, have been just the opposite of you. Perhaps I was just curious to discover what a man like you had to offer...'

'A man like me...'

'You know...tall, dark, handsome, powerful, the essence

of every teenage fantasy.' She sneaked a sideways glance at him from lowered lashes and shivered at the icy expression on his face.

But she had to do what she had to do. To protect herself. Or else she would find herself as putty in his hands, taken and then discarded, and she knew that she was just not sophisticated or world-weary enough to deal with the heartache that would inevitably follow. What ingrained expertise and control she possessed was reserved for her working side. Her emotional side, as she was fast learning, was full of holes.

'I see.'

'We're both adults, these things happen. I just think we should put it all down to experience.'

He could still feel the melting compliance of her body against his, could still taste the sweetness of her mouth on his own, and here she was, talking about *putting the whole thing down to experience*! Riccardo wanted to believe that fear and not reason was talking, fear at how he had made her feel, fear that she might find herself in the grip of a passion she could not control, but alongside that wish was a nasty seed of doubt. Julia Nash was not like the other women he had known. Of that she was absolutely right. He could not read her. He might guess at what went on in her head, but he could not be sure.

And he would certainly never run after a woman who spoke of curiosity and experience, even if his gut instinct was telling him to disbelieve what his ears heard and go only on what his eyes read.

His pride slammed into place and he turned on the engine, the tyres screeching as he manoeuvred his car out of its slot and headed towards the exit.

'So we've both had an experience,' he said mockingly, 'and now where does that leave us?'

Julia had not thought that far ahead. As always, he was one step in front of her. She remembered they were still playing a game, still hanging on to the pretence that they were dating, so that he could have easy, frequent access to Nicola, until the time was right for their relationship to assume its natural course.

Her mouth went dry with apprehension. It would mean seeing him, being in his company.

'Perhaps we should tell Nicola the truth now,' she said quietly. 'Tell her that you're her father, and that way we can forget about this farcical pretence about going out.'

Riccardo laughed sardonically. 'Oh, I see. The time is right now because it suits you, is that it? Now that your adolescent fantasies have been satisfied, you're happy to break the news to my daughter, even if she might not be emotionally ready to accept such a revelation.'

He braked at a traffic light and she could see the harsh set of his face.

'She knows you now. It's not as if she's seeing you for the first time,' Julia argued.

'She lost her mother only months ago, and the only man she ever regarded as a father figure. Suddenly, you intend to tell her that no, we weren't going out, because I have appeared on the scene and she's to accept me. And you think she won't go scurrying into her shell? You think the trust she's building with me won't evaporate overnight?'

'I'm doing you a favour!' Julia heard the plea in her voice and felt a rush of panic.

'You mean you're doing *yourself* a favour!' He glanced across at her, his black eyes glittering. 'Well, it won't work.'

'What do you mean?'

'I mean that *I* am calling the shots here and *I* don't think the time is right. Whether you like it or not, we're going to carry on playing the devoted couple.'

He sped off from the traffic lights, barely hesitating as he manoeuvred along the streets and around roundabouts.

'And how long do you think that is going to take?'

'How long is a piece of string?'

Julia stared, unseeing, through the window and tried to imagine the agony of being in his presence and having to laugh and chat as though he had not rocked her to the very foundations of her being. Ironic insofar as that had been his intention, she thought bitterly. If only he knew.

'In fact,' he said slowly, 'we can't be too far away from the Easter school holidays. When are they, exactly?'

Julia gave him the dates, wondering what he had in mind. She had no need to ask the question.

'It might be an ideal opportunity for her to get to know a bit of Italy. She could meet some of her relatives over there. Naturally, I would expect you to come along as well, to ease the ground, so to speak.'

'That's impossible.'

'Nothing in life is impossible. Haven't you grasped that that is my motto and one I have always stuck by?'

'And what if one of us finds another partner before then?' Julia threw at him. As far as she was concerned, it was a far-fetched notion but the only one she could think of that might put a spoke in the devil's wheel, but far from seeming disconcerted he simply gave a dry laugh.

'You mean, what if I bump into one of those blondes to whom I apparently have no resistance?'

'I mean, what if *I* meet someone?' Julia flung back at him, and a thick silence ensued, which she feverishly felt was laden with implied disbelief. God, he must have thought that he could snap his fingers and she would jump, because she was no stunner. And was it any wonder that he had felt that way? After the impression her mother had inadvertently given him? The impression of a retiring girl, housebound because of her duties to her five-year-old niece, who rarely left the house? No wonder he had taken her to a nightclub. He probably thought that he would show her a little action and perk her life up. In more ways than one! She gritted her teeth in frustration.

'Oh,' he said softly, 'but how easy is it going to be to go running back to your predictable line of sensitive, domesticated males? You yourself admitted that they are not the object of any woman's fantasy…'

'Why, you are so damned *conceited*…!' Julia spluttered. 'And that's not what I said at all!'

Riccardo shrugged dismissively. 'Besides, you are not at liberty to do anything with anyone at the moment. Your duty is at my side, holding my hand and putting on a very convincing performance for the sake of my child.'

She hadn't realised how much ground they had covered and how quickly until the car slowed down and she saw that they were pulling into the short drive that led to the house, which was in darkness. She looked at her watch and realised, with astonishment, that the hours had slipped by. It was now after one and, strangely enough, she was not in the least tired. In fact, she had never felt more wide awake.

'Which, I believe, will be tomorrow? To take *both* of you to the zoo? Where you will laugh and give every semblance of being thrilled to be in my company.' He leant across to open her door and in the process his arm brushed her breasts, which tingled at the brief contact. She was certain that he had done that deliberately but Julia wasn't going to argue the point. She pushed open the door and scuttled out of the car, almost tripping in her haste to get to the front door.

'You needn't see me in,' she muttered, rummaging in her bag for the key.

'I wouldn't dream of driving off and leaving you on your doorstep. What kind of man would I be?'

'The kind of man you've proven yourself to be,' Julia retorted.

'You've already admitted that you used me,' he said coolly, 'so perhaps, then, we're better suited than you think.'

'I doubt it.'

A flicker of something shadowed his face, but his voice was neutral when he next spoke, asking her what time he could come and collect them the following day.

'After lunch,' Julia told him, feeling hunted. 'Around one-thirty. That will give us time to eat.'

'In which case I shall join you for lunch. I'll see you at twelve.'

Julia could hardly concentrate the following morning. Everywhere she turned, she caught images of herself and Riccardo. She had had a very long bath the previous night, or rather early morning, when she had returned home, but nothing could wash away the musky scent on her, the scent of a satisfied woman. Her thoughts haunted her, teasing her with remembered pleasure and then admonishing her for her insanity. And the more insane her behaviour seemed, the more coolly calculating his own appeared.

She was a bag of nerves by the time he arrived promptly at twelve for lunch, but his behaviour was impeccable. There were no allusions, not even on the odd occasion when they found themselves in the same room without either Nicola or her mother around, to what had happened the night before.

Disconcertingly, his silence on the subject only served to reconfirm her impression that their lovemaking had been a spontaneous but miscalculated error of judgement, at least on his part. He had given in to the temptation of appeasing his sexual curiosity about her and was now content to play his part without batting an eyelid.

The same could not have been said of Julia. She was agonisingly aware of him, and even when they touched in passing she could feel her body react, as though it had a life of its own, quite independent of the workings of her brain.

Her fiery little outburst about finding someone else, said in the heat of the moment to scupper his smugness that she would fall in with whatever he had in mind, for however long it took, had obviously been dismissed as ridiculous.

It was an unutterable relief when they wearily made their way back to the house, with Nicola chatting happily between them in the taxi.

'You can relax now,' Riccardo said, following her into the house and closing the door behind him.

'I wasn't tense,' Julia lied, with her back to him. 'I suppose you must be getting on your way now.' She turned around and looked pointedly at the door.

Wasn't tense? Riccardo thought that he could have had quite an argument with her about that, but it would have been an argument going in circles. For every one step forward with her, he took five back, and the amazing thing was that he was still determined to put another foot in front.

Why?

He was better equipped to understand his motives for revenge, dubious though they had been. Revenge was a violent, passionate emotion in tune with his soul. But he no longer wanted any kind of revenge and the truth was that he was no longer sure what he wanted.

Except he wanted Julia. And he was determined that he would have her again. This time, though, his approach would not be one of physical persuasion, but something far more subtle. He shook his head to clear it of the buzzing hornet's nest that was driving him mad.

'I'll have a cup of coffee before I go.'

'Is that one of your orders?'

'It's a request,' he told her, in a voice that matched hers. 'Look, we've had a good day. Why don't we call a truce?'

Julia didn't answer but preceded him into the kitchen, to find Nicola getting out her colouring book, one that had been bought for her from the souvenir shop at the zoo.

'I'll colour with you later, honey,' Julia said, nervously aware that Riccardo was watching her. She almost tipped hot water over her hand under the casual, brooding scrutiny.

'I don't know if you want to see Nicola during the week,' she began quietly, edging towards the far end of the kitchen, away from idle ears. 'If not, next weekend would be fine, although not on Saturday evening. I won't be around.'

'Won't you? Where are you going?'

'Out.' A friend had invited her to a birthday party and Julia was looking forward to it. She had not seen Elizabeth in nearly two months and there would be other mutual friends there as well. It would be blissfully relaxing not to have Riccardo around like a burr under her skin.

'Out where?' His voice was hard and Julia met his stare levelly.

'None of your business, Riccardo. I *have* got a private life, you know, even though you might not want to believe it.'

'Cancel whoever it is you are seeing. I want to take you both out to dinner on Saturday.'

'Forget it.' She could have told him the occasion, knew that he would understand because underneath his aggression she was all too familiar with a side of him that was scrupulously fair, even though it might not always pertain to her. But a sudden wicked urge incited her to keep him guessing. 'I'm not changing my plans.'

Riccardo watched the shuttered expression as she sipped her coffee and a cold, icy rage wafted through him. He couldn't believe it. She was going out with a man. No woman looked like that, expression veiled, unless she was holding a secret to herself, and the only secrets women did not share with their lovers, because lovers they had been and would be again, was the presence on the scene of another lover.

Jealousy ripped through him, leaving him shaken. A pulse in his jaw began to beat fiercely and he lowered his eyes.

'Why not? Are your plans that important?' The words were dragged out of him. He knew that he should stop now but he couldn't.

'Very important,' Julia answered truthfully. 'I haven't seen this particular friend for quite a while now and I'm very much looking forward to meeting up.' She drained her coffee and thought, Well, I have a life and you can put that in your pipe and smoke it.

And she could see that he didn't like it, didn't like not being obeyed.

Perhaps, she thought in a blinding flash, the time was coming for her to change. To stop driving in the slow lane while everyone else was in the fast.

'I have changed my mind,' Riccardo said abruptly as jealousy stroked his mind with icy fingers.

'Changed your mind? What about?'

He glanced at Nicola and then stared broodingly at the woman in front of him.

No more pretences, dammit. He wanted Julia and now he would pursue her without the dubious advantage of knowing that her hands were tied, that she was compelled to wear a smile to fuel the illusion of a relationship in the eyes of his unknowing daughter. All of that suddenly seemed like the cheap tactics of a coward and coward he most certainly was not.

The time had come for honesty to prevail.

'Nicola,' he said softly, squatting so that he was on her level as she approached him. 'There's something I have to say to you.'

'Riccardo!'

'No, Julia. No more pretence.'

'But I thought—'

'It's time.'

'Time for what?' Nicola looked at them, frowning and Riccardo smiled tenderly and absorbed one of her small hands in his.

'Time to tell you, my sweet, that you have at least three people that love you very much, Aunty Jules, and Grandma and...' His voice wavered and Julia laid her hand on his shoulder, knowing that their shared strength would be important for Nicola.

'And...me.'

'What do you mean?'

'I mean that I am your dad, my child.'

There was an agonisingly long silence, or so it seemed to Julia, then Nicola smiled, a little shadow of a smile that was tinged with shyness.

'My *real* dad?'

'Your real dad,' Riccardo said gravely, his heart bursting as the smile enfolded him.

'I knew...'

'You *knew*? That I was your dad?'

'That you would come back to find me.'

CHAPTER SEVEN

JULIA looked at her reflection in the full-length mirror in her bedroom and didn't know whether to be shocked, thrilled or just confused at what confronted her. Over the past week, she had worked on her self-image with the fast and furious pace of someone fleeing from the devil. Which just about summed it up as far as she was concerned. Riccardo Fabbrini was the devil and she was fleeing from him and straight into the arms of a damage-limitation exercise which would give her strength and propel her into the sort of life which she felt she needed desperately if she wasn't to fall deeper into the quagmire of her confused emotions.

She needed to prove to him, once and for all, that she was no walkover to be used and discarded at his pleasure. She refused to be the brown sparrow to his circling hawk. And more than that: his role was now complete. He had told Nicola of his true identity and her heart wrenched as she imagined her niece's gradual withdrawal from her life. She *needed* to move on now.

On the Monday she had gone to her optician's. Having always worn spectacles, she had listened to Nick Healey's sales patter on the convenience of contact lenses with scepticism, and was even more sceptical when informed that with soft contact lenses there would be little if any initial discomfort. She had returned for her lenses three days later and had overcome her queasiness at the thought of putting a foreign object into her eye by reminding herself that it was all for a greater purpose.

In between ordering her lenses and having them fitted, Julia took herself to the hairdresser's after work. Her usual unexciting wash, shampoo, trim and blow dry was replaced by a dramatic blunt bob that fell thickly to chin level, and a complete dye job, with highlights. She was now the proud possessor, for the first time in her life, of a hair colour that was not her own. Rich chestnut with golden auburn highlights.

Julia spent the remainder of the week shopping. She ignored the temptation to throw her money in the direction of the most background outfits with the least daring cuts and staunchly headed for the overpowering sales assistants who eyed her body knowingly and were only too overjoyed to clothe her in short, adventurous designs in striking colours.

Now, barely a week later, Julia stood in front of the mirror and looked at the completed job. She looked much taller and a lot more shapely than she had imagined herself to be. Her hair swung provocatively around her face, a riot of carefully blended colours and without spectacles her eyes were clearly visible for the first time. Large grey eyes, shadowed with a subtle application of eye make-up.

And, to complete the show, her new pale blue, very short skirt and matching jacket that was tailored to emphasise every line of her slender body. Under the jacket, a small, tight top clung to her like a second skin. Her shoes were black and high and undeniably sexy.

Julia did a twirl and thought that she looked the part, if she didn't exactly feel it.

But looking was good enough for her. Let Riccardo Fabbrini see that she was a force to be reckoned with, that she was not some sad, desperate woman who found it impossible not to respond to his polished, experienced charm and fabulous good looks.

Shame it was all about to be wasted on a girlfriend's birthday party, but then again, she thought wryly, a bit of practice might help when it came to the niggling technicalities of sitting in minuscule skirts and walking in three-inch heels.

She glanced at her delicate bracelet watch, a present from her parents when she was sixteen and the only item with which she had refused to part company. Her mother would be here in an hour to babysit, although Nicola was already in bed at a little after seven, and then she would launch herself into the world.

She had just peeked in to see Nicola and give her a final goodnight kiss, when the doorbell rang.

Now this, Julia thought with a grin, will take a little getting used to. Sashaying. Something she had never done before. She sashayed down the stairs, resisting the impulse to remove her shoes and run down the way she usually did, and pulled open the door with a wide smile, waiting for her mother's shocked reaction.

The expression froze on her face as she absorbed who was standing on the doorstep, his hands thrust into his pockets.

'What are *you* doing here?' Julia stood in front of him, barricading his entry, one hand on her hip, the other holding the door ajar.

Riccardo recovered quickly from the gut punch he had felt on seeing her. So he had been right, he thought savagely. Out on a date with a man and dressed to kill for the occasion. Looking every inch a knock-out. His black eyes travelled the length of her body, lingering on her legs and the jut of her breasts under the cling-film top she was wearing. When he finally met her eyes it was to find her looking at him coldly.

'I asked you what you were doing here,' Julia repeated.

Never had she been so blatantly stripped before and she was angry to find that the mental striptease had turned her cool confidence into heated arousal.

But her appearance, she thought fiercely, was now her armour, and she remained where she was, not flinching.

'I've come to babysit,' Riccardo answered, his mouth twisting. 'I have every right, considering I am Nicola's father and there are no flimsy pretences remaining between me and my child.'

'That's impossible. Mum's babysitting,' Julia replied. 'In fact, she should be here any minute now.'

'Should be but won't. Because I phoned to let her know that as I am free tonight, I would take over. Now, are you going to stand aside and let me in or do I have to push past you and let myself in?'

Julia stood aside, furious, and waited until he was in before slamming the door behind her. 'How dare you?' she said in a low, strangled voice. 'How dare you re-arrange my plans so that you can come here and *check up on me*?'

'Check up on you? I'm doing nothing of the sort. I'm helping out. Where is my daughter?'

'Upstairs. Asleep.'

'Very wise.'

'And what is *that* supposed to mean?'

His eyes did another indolent appraisal of her body and Julia felt another wave of heat wash over her.

'It means that you did the sensible thing in making sure that my daughter does not see her surrogate mother going out dressed like a tart!' He knew that every word he was saying was getting under her skin and that every lazy glance over her barely dressed body was enraging her, and he felt a vicious sense of satisfaction. Let her go out raging, let her spend her romantic evening furiously thinking about *him*.

'I am *not* dressed like a tart,' Julia hissed furiously. She glanced up the stairs and then pulled him by his jacket out of the hall and away from any possibility of being seen by Nicola should she just happen to wake up and stroll out of her bedroom at the wrong moment.

'That skirt barely covers you. And where are your spectacles? If you don't fall flat on your face in those heels then you'll trip over something, and how elegant are you going to look in front of your man?'

'I'm wearing contact lenses,' Julia said tersely. 'Not that it's any of your business.'

'It damn well *is* my business! I will not allow my daughter to see you in a get-up like the one you're wearing! What the hell sort of example do you imagine you are setting?' God, he sounded positively Victorian but, dammit, he wanted to strip her of those wickedly provocative clothes. Just the thought of some man looking at her, daring to let his gaze linger over the swell of her breasts and that ripely deep-pink mouth, wonder what the body was like under the cling film, was enough to make him clench his jaw in a possessive fury.

'I will wear what I like, Riccardo.' She strode across to pick up her jacket which she had draped over the banister and slung it on defiantly, then snatched her small clutch bag from the table in the hall.

'Not if I have anything to do with it,' he growled. What exactly he *could* do about it was beyond his comprehension, and his impotence only served to add tinder to the fire. 'This is not the sort of example I want to have set for my child!'

Julia looked at him in frank amazement. 'Since when did you have such a highly developed puritanical streak, Riccardo Fabbrini? From the look of your last girlfriend, it must be a very recently acquired trait!'

'Helen was my lover; my child was not in her care. If she had been then rest assured I would not have allowed her to dress like a wh—'

'Don't even think about saying it,' Julia said in an icy voice. 'I'm going now and I'll be back in a few hours' time. You know where everything is.'

She turned and as she was opening the door felt his hand descend on her arm, forcing her to turn and face him.

'Where are you going, anyway?' he demanded, his eyes clashing with hers. A man could lose himself in those eyes. Clever, suspicious, bruised eyes that could trap a man. *Who the hell was she going out with?*

'That's none of your business!'

'And what if I need to get in touch with you? What if Nicola wakes up and asks after you? She might be disoriented. What if she falls ill?'

'I have my mobile phone with me.' Julia glanced around for a piece of paper and a pencil, glared at him and then began sashaying towards the kitchen. The tightness of the skirt combined with the height of her heels made her feel headily provocative, even though she was steaming angry at his high-handed attitude. But there was nothing to be done. She had to give him her phone number despite the fact that it was extremely unlikely that it would be needed.

She could feel his eyes boring into her as he followed her and it seemed to take several hours covering ground between the hall and the kitchen. How on earth did women maintain this look all the time? Did they get used to the heels or did they just resign themselves to walking very, very slowly for the sake of their vanity?

'Here's my mobile number.' She handed him a piece of paper, which he didn't glance at, just shoved in his pocket while he continued to stare at her blackly. 'Though I don't think you'll need it,' Julia informed him, clicking her way out of the kitchen and back to the front door. 'Nicola was exhausted tonight and she very rarely wakes up once she goes to sleep. And you're her father! I don't think she'll be alarmed if she does get up and finds you here instead of her grandma.'

'And what time do you intend to be back?' If any woman had ever questioned his movements the way he was questioning hers, he knew that he would have hit the roof, but he didn't give a damn if he sounded like an inquisitor.

'I'll be back when I'm back,' Julia informed him. She was beginning to enjoy the sensation of watching him squirm in his own discomfort and had absolutely no inclination to disabuse him of the illusion that she was going out with a man. Not that she was strictly telling a lie, she thought. There *would* be men at the party, although probably all of the safely married variety. 'In other words,' she added sweetly, 'don't wait up for me. You could try watching a little telly. There's a very good period drama on you might enjoy. You'll be able to identify with some of the men. They're overbearing and unreasonable as well.'

'With a tongue like yours,' Riccardo told her, flushing darkly as the accuracy of her remark hit home, 'you'll be back within the hour. Men don't appreciate sarcasm in their women.'

'You mean *you* don't appreciate sarcasm in *your* women,' she amended, pausing with her hand on the door and looking up at him. The beautiful, tearful Helen certainly had not seemed to be the sort of woman who spoke back, and Caroline had been as meek as a lamb. No wonder she had spent her marriage in a state of nervous tension.

'And you're telling me that the man you're going to be seeing *does*?' Riccardo gave a crack of derisory laughter that set her teeth on edge. If he hadn't been so damned unreasonable she thought that she might just have told him the truth, but his remarks about her appearance had hurt. Not once had he said that she looked good. He had insulted her from the very minute he had walked through the door.

'I'll have to wait and see, won't I?'

'I thought you were only interested in *nice men*,' Riccardo sneered. 'You'll send your *nice man* running for cover within minutes!'

'I'm going now.' Julia turned the door knob and offered him a bright smile.

He ignored her. His dark brows met in a thunderous frown and Julia responded by gazing serenely back at him. He could have killed her. Men were men, he thought savagely, and it would be easy for any nice man to turn into a wolf, given the goods on offer. God, he could see every curve of her body under what she was wearing and the exposure of her legs was positively indecent.

'Before you go,' he said, lowering his voice, 'I'll just give you something to think about, shall I? You'll want to know how your nice little man holds up to the competition.' And he pulled her towards him, his mouth descending to crush against hers. It was a hot, brutal kiss that made every nerve in her body leap. For the most fleeting of seconds, she responded. She had to. Then she struggled against him and he released her immediately, but not without affording her a look of pure triumph.

'I'll see you soon,' he drawled mockingly.

Julia turned away and let herself out of the house in a blind rush. How could he manage to do that? How could he manage to overwhelm her when he hadn't even been *pleasant*? The minute his mouth had touched hers she had felt herself falling and it had taken all the strength she could muster to pull her back. How could she have fallen in love with a man whose arrogance knew no bounds and who could be ruthless and charming in equal measure? Love should be gentle, a soothing meeting of minds, not this mad, roller-coaster ride that left her spending half her time in a state of anguished giddiness!

And he had been right. The memory of his kiss had ruined her enjoyment of the evening because she found that she could hardly focus on what was going on around her. She was dimly aware of compliments being lavished on her and of several men who left her in no doubt that they liked what they saw. One in particular was so bowled over that he pressed his name and telephone number into her hand as she was leaving.

'Call me,' he urged, while her friend made funny faces behind his back and gave her the thumbs-up sign. 'I work in the City. It would be no problem meeting up after work, or even meeting for lunch. I can easily arrange to come to you.' He was fair, good-looking and undeniably *nice*. Just the sort of man Julia knew she should be cultivating. In her old get-up of plain skirts and concealing tops, it was doubtful whether he would have given her a second look, but his blue eyes had been on stalks every time he had looked at her during the course of the evening.

'Perhaps,' Julia answered vaguely, backing away from the eagerness in his expression.

'What about next week? Give me your phone number and I can call you; see if we can touch base.' He was so insistent, and Julia was so desperate to wriggle out of being forced into committing herself to anything, that she hurriedly rattled off her home number, hoping that his memory would fail him. Not that he couldn't find out where she was and her telephone number if he wanted. Elizabeth would be more than obliging. She had spent half the evening telling Julia about his eligibility! Brilliant job, no messy divorce behind him, kind to children and animals, thoroughly nice guy.

Unfortunately, Julia's mouth was still burning from the kiss of a thoroughly *un*-nice guy!

But it was lovely being the object of flattery, and she returned home at a little after midnight, far more cheerful than when she had set out.

The house, when she arrived, was in darkness, which surprised her. She hadn't thought that Riccardo was the sort of man who retired early to bed. Which left her in the uncomfortable position of knowing that if he was asleep she would either have to wake him up or else let him carry on sleeping, and if she allowed him to carry on sleeping she would spend the rest of the night tossing and turning in bed, knowing that he was under the same roof.

She threw her little clutch bag on the table in the hall, clicking her teeth in frustration, and went through the downstairs rooms, checking them one by one to make sure that he wasn't in any of them.

The last was the small sitting room where the television was, which, like the rest of the rooms, was in complete darkness. Julia was about to shut the door when his dark, velvety voice addressed her from the direction of one of the chairs.

'Don't do that!' she said, still shaking from the fright he had given her.

'Don't do what?'

'You made me jump. What are you doing sitting here in the dark, anyway?' She switched on the light and saw him sprawled comfortably on one of the deep chairs, his long legs extended in front of him.

Riccardo could have told her that he had found it suited his mood but he didn't. Anyway, he was in quite good humour now. In fact, feeling amazingly contented. So instead, he pointedly looked at his watch and then at her face.

'Has Nicola been all right?' Julia hovered in the doorway, not too sure what she should do. Throw him out? Hint that it was time to go? Chat politely and wait for him to leave of his own accord? Maybe, she considered, she should offer him the going rate for babysitting and see what he did. The thought made her grin.

'Nicola's been fine, and what's so funny? Care to share the joke with me?'

'Oh, I was just thinking about this evening…'

'Had a good time, did you?'

'I had a brilliant time.' She looked at him, giving him the opportunity to stand up and leave, and when he remained sitting she reluctantly enquired politely, 'What did you do?'

Riccardo shrugged and threw her a lazy smile. A lazy, *genuine* smile, which made her narrow her eyes suspiciously at him. He looked a little too much like the cat that had got the cream for her liking.

'Oh, watched a little television. Didn't think much of that period drama you recommended. Not enough action. There was a much better film on another channel so I looked at that. On and off.'

Julia remained standing, arms folded, taking full advantage of her one-off situation of looking down at *him* instead of the other way around.

'Oh, and I grabbed something to eat. Hope you don't mind. Just a sandwich.'

'That's fine.'

He gave her a dazzling smile and relaxed a little deeper into his chair, resting his head back against his clasped hands, seeming unperturbed by the wariness stamped on her face. On her eminently kissable face, he thought, not that she was aware of that. Her superficial change of plumage would never be able to eradicate her innate modesty, however much she tried to camouflage it.

'So…' he said, raising his eyebrows, 'where did you go…?'

'Oh, nowhere out of the ordinary. The company is what counts,' she added meaningfully, and he gave her another brilliant smile, nodding in agreement. 'Anyway, I guess you must be tired…so, if you don't mind…'

'Oh, I'm not tired. It's only twelve-thirty. I have a body clock that relishes the minimum amount of sleep.'

'Well, bully for you. I don't.'

'And I thought we might have a cosy little chat.'

'A cosy little chat? What about?'

'About where you *really* were tonight, of course.' Riccardo almost wanted to purr with satisfaction. The thought of her being with another man had driven him almost mad with rage. Male pride, he assumed. No one liked to be walked out on, least of all a man like him. Deplorable, but at least, he thought, he had had the honesty to admit to the trait. Rage over nothing, as it had turned out.

'Get to the point, Riccardo.'

'In between the action movie, the sandwich and two glasses of wine—I hope you don't mind my raiding your fridge—I found some time to call your mother…'

'You found some time *to do what*?' So much for her provocative subterfuge, intended to leave him in no doubt that he was dismissible at the click of her fingers because she had another man waiting in the wings. She sat down and looked at him, her cheeks pink with guilt at what she knew was coming.

'Oh, to telephone your mother. I couldn't remember where I had put that piece of paper with your mobile-phone number on it and, naturally, I had to find out how I could contact you just in case…' He threw her a pious smile. 'Your mother was most obliging. In fact, we had a pleasant little chat. Seems that your hot date with a mystery man was in fact a birthday party at your girlfriend's house...'

'I never said I was going on a hot date with anyone...' Julia denied hotly. '*You* jumped to the conclusion that I was and—'

'You let me go along with the misapprehension...the burning question is *why*...'

'It's time you left.' Julia sat forward, flicked open her little bag and extracted her bundle of keys. Her skin felt as though it was on fire, a tingling sensation induced by the fact that she felt cornered, and was all too aware of what further conclusions he might be leaping towards in answer to his own question.

She could see it written all over that smug, breathtakingly handsome face of his. He thought that she had deliberately lied to make him jealous, and why would she want to make him jealous? Because she was violently attracted to him. She dangled the keys from her fingers and stood up.

'It's late, Riccardo, and I'm tired. I don't need to sit here and answer any of your questions!'

'Scared?'

'Scared of what? Of you? You don't intimidate me in the slightest, Riccardo Fabbrini!'

'What about scared of owning up to the truth?'

Julia didn't dare ask him to clarify his remark. She had a sinking feeling that she wasn't going to like what else he had to say on the subject and she could already feel her own arguments ringing hollowly in the room as she tried to convince him otherwise.

'Now, why don't you go and get us both a cup of coffee and we can discuss this?'

'There's nothing to discuss!'

Riccardo shot her a politely incredulous smile and Julia

feverishly wondered what the punishment was for manslaughter. 'Of course there is,' he said calmly. 'Now, shall I tell you the way I see it?'

Julia sat back down, heaved a huge sigh and rolled her eyes heavenwards. 'I would rather you didn't, but I don't suppose that will stop you.'

'Quite true.' He appeared to give the matter careful consideration. 'Well, the way I see it is like this. You want me. That much is obvious, and don't look at me as though you haven't got the faintest idea what I'm talking about. You know exactly what I'm talking about, although if you like I can always remind you of the last evening we spent together…? In the space of one week—in fact, since you met that last girlfriend of mine—you've undergone a few radical changes. Not, I might add, that you didn't turn me on before—'

'I never turned you on, Riccardo Fabbrini! You used me!'

Riccardo shook his head sadly, as if despairing of a child being wilfully obtuse. 'Men don't work like that. You can think what you like about my motives, but no man can pretend passion. Oh, I wanted you all right. You felt it.' His voice was a low, sexy murmur that had the blood rushing to her cheeks. 'I was big and hard for you and that's not something a man can summon to order…'

'Riccardo…' Julia heard the weak desperation in her voice and wanted to groan at her own lack of will power in the face of this fascinating, unbearably sexy man.

'You don't have to feel that you're in competition with Helen or any of the other blonde airheads I've dated in the past.'

'I don't feel anything of the sort!' Her eyes flashed at him. Water off a duck's back.

'Or that you have to pretend to be going out with another man so that you can fire me up…'

'You…You are so…'

'I know, I know. Arrogant, conceited et cetera, et cetera. But accurate, no? So, what do we do with this…shall we say…passion of ours…?'

Julia stared at him, open-mouthed. This must be how it felt to toss a boomerang into the air, only for it to return and hit you straight on the face. At the party she had been the essence of poise and self-control. She had been able to have conversations with men without even paying them the slightest bit of attention. Fifteen minutes in this man's company and it was all blown to smithereens! Could this really be love?

The only clear thought running through her chaotic brain now was not to let him see just how much she felt and how powerless she was to resist him. For all his talk about passion and wanting and whether he had used her for his own purposes or not, he was a man incapable of giving with his soul. He could give magnificently with his body, but in her heart Julia knew that that would never be enough for her.

'I don't want to talk about any of this,' she breathed.

'You mean talk about us sleeping together? Giving in to this craving we have to touch each other's bodies?' Just talking about this and looking at her as she sat forward, pink-faced and rapt, wanting so badly to run but held captive by his voice, was enough to make him go hard.

She stared at him in silence. Every exit seemed to be blocked. She *hadn't* been trying to rouse his jealousy…had she? she wondered wildly. She had been trying to build up her own confidence in herself, to prove to him that she was not the pushover she must have seemed to be when she had swooned in his arms like a mindless Victorian maiden. She had changed her image because, obscurely, she had wanted to change the disastrous direction her life appeared to have been taking. Straight into his bed! Leaving her heart in tattered pieces when he was through with her! *That* was what she had been trying to do, except pointing all that out to him would be like running in circles.

'Look,' he said with sudden fierceness, sitting forward and filling the spaces around her with his overpowering masculinity, 'do you imagine I want to feel this way too? You detonated a bombshell in my life; you're the last person in the world I should be wanting to take to my bed, but I feel the same thing that you do!'

'You're mistaken,' Julia said in a shaky voice, standing up. Her legs didn't feel as though they could support her suddenly leaden body, but she had to get out of the room. 'I just thought that the time had come for me to take control of my life, that's all.'

'Make us both some coffee and you can tell me all about it. You'll find that I am a very good listener.'

Any excuse. She scurried out of the room and into the kitchen, where she leaned against the counter and closed her eyes. Everything inside her was pounding, her heart, her brain, her whole body felt as though it could burst through its skin.

Want, want, want. He wanted her, wanted to sleep with her, make love. It was all that mattered to him. But it wasn't enough. She wearily put the kettle to boil, her movements automatic as she piled a teaspoon of instant coffee into each mug, poured the water over, but her hands were shaking when she went to lift the mugs and she had to set them down again while she caught herself and took a few deep breaths. She might deter him for the moment, but he was like a shark that had suddenly discovered a source of blood. Hers!

And now that Nicola knew who he was, he was under

no obligation to hang around. He would take what he *wanted* and then he would be gone, with his daughter.

She was leaning against the counter, thinking madly of how she could extricate herself from the situation in one piece, how she could resist the temptation to cave in to both their needs because caving in would be the fatal step towards heartbreak. She barely heard his approaching steps.

When he spoke his voice was deadly icy and her eyes flickered open to see him standing in front of her, a piece of paper in his hand.

'What is this?' He held the paper out to her, and without thinking Julia asked him whether he had finally discovered the whereabouts of the missing mobile-phone number. Not that she had believed for one minute that he had really misplaced it.

'Look at it.' He thrust the paper at her and Julia was dimly aware that he had found the piece of paper with Roger's telephone number on it. At the time, she had barely glanced at it, but now she could see that he had inscribed a rough heart under the phone number.

'Where did you find this?'

'Does it matter?' He folded his arms and waited. Waited till her eyes had finished scanning the paper for a second time. 'I found it.'

'You had no right to go prying in my bag,' she said quietly.

'The damn bag was open from when you got your keys out! I saw the edge of paper sticking out and yes, I took it out and now I want to know who the hell this Roger person is and why his telephone number is in your bag!'

'You have no right to question me on—'

'I have every right!'

Every right, Julia thought, to be furious because his idea of a few nights of passion before he tossed her aside had been thwarted. Through the murky light, she began to see a glimmer of hope, a way out of the mess which would put her beyond his reach. Not to seize it would be folly. She knew, they both did, that, however much she might try to run, his pursuit would be successful, but if he thought that there was another man he would be forced to leave her alone and that way she would be free to retreat, to lick her wounds in private and thank the lord that they were not more severe.

And she was as free now as he was. There was no longer any reason to pretend a relationship. She could do precisely as she pleased!

'I met him at the party.' Julia stole a defiant look at his thunderous face and her eyes skittered away nervously. 'I thought it was going to be a small do, but it turned out to be quite large. A lot of Elizabeth's husband's friends were there. Roger was one of them.' His cold silence was making her ramble on. 'He…he's a stockbroker in the City. He was very interesting and when I was l-lea…leaving he gave me his telephone number. I… Riccardo, stop looking at me like that! It's not a crime to chat to a man at a party, or to take his phone number, for that matter…'

'Was that the intention when you left this house this evening? In your short skirt and high heels? To chat up any man you came across?'

'I did not *chat him up*! He chatted me up! And that wasn't my intention! I'm not the sort of girl who goes to parties to see who they can pull!' The idea was so ridiculous that in another situation she would have burst out laughing at the image he was portraying of her as some kind of vamp who flirted her way round the men until she found a suitable candidate.

'So let me get this straight. You've changed your appearance. Now you wear clothes that barely cover your body, and in addition you're willing to offer yourself to the first man that comes along and gives you a line about wanting to get to know you.' His mouth twisted into a sardonic scowl, but before Julia could open her mouth to protest he had picked up the thread of his accusation and was hurtling forward with it, giving her no time to think, let alone speak.

'And you want me to believe that this is the sort of example I want my daughter to be set? I don't think so.'

'You're being ridiculous, Riccardo.' But her protest was thin, simply because he had a way of twisting things to suit his arguments. Twisting *her* until she didn't know what she was saying or doing or thinking!

'I am not being ridiculous. Nor am I being ridiculous when I inform you that there is only one way to deal with this.'

'Wh-what way…?'

'Well, put it this way…I won't disrupt Nicola so soon after telling her who I am by removing her from her familiar surroundings. So…'

'So…?'

'So I am going to move in here with you.'

CHAPTER EIGHT

RICCARDO gazed out of the massive floor-to-ceiling window in his office and stared down at the busy, teeming London streets eleven storeys below. It was a view which, in the past, had afforded him a great deal of pleasure. To be in his large, plush office with its black leather and thick-piled carpet, to know that the entire glass building in which he stood and which dominated everything else around it belonged to him.

His family had begged him to return to Italy, especially after he had married Caroline, but it had been the only thing she had ever refused to do and secretly he had been delighted by the get-out clause her adamant refusal had given him. Because he had loved the vast concrete jungle that was London, had revelled in his relentless and satisfying climb into the rarefied reaches of true power. And after their bitter split he had thrown himself into his work with even more gusto. Nothing and no one, none of the blondes who had nurtured hopes of taming the beast, had provided even the slightest breath of competition when it came to where his attention was focused.

He sighed now with frustration and raked his fingers through his black hair as he contemplated how much things had changed in the space of a few short weeks.

Nicola was the mainspring of that change and one he welcomed. Fatherhood, delayed as it had been, was a joyous addition to his life. But she was only part of the equation.

He scowled as his mind began its familiar and invasive

exploration of Julia. In a short while he would begin the process of collating vital files and computer discs that he would be transferring to her house. He had already arranged for a computer terminal, a separate telephone line and a fax machine to be set up there. She would return from school to find him fully installed. The heady thrill of power and the frantic pace of life within the cool, elegant confines of his superb office no longer held the allure they once had.

Just the thought of her with her new look and her new hair and her legs on view for all to see, just the thought of her stepping out into the London social scene with that extraordinary appeal of innocence and sexiness threw him into panicked rage and consumed his every waking moment. Not to mention the appearance of some man, some stockbroker with octopus hands and sticky fingers.

Riccardo's jaw clenched and he began prowling through the office, sifting through his files, selecting some, leaving the rest. By eleven o'clock he was ready to leave, only stopping *en route* to remind his secretary that he would be available via e-mail, phone or fax and would continue to come into the office, albeit with less regularity. He knew that she was utterly bewildered by his decision to work more from home but he offered no explanation. He had called an emergency board meeting the previous day and had announced the same decision and had met a similar barrier of utter incomprehension, but they had rallied around quickly, moving with speed and efficiency into their extended roles. He had always surrounded himself with quick thinking, ambitious men and they had risen to the occasion admirably. A fat bonus to accommodate any extra duties had helped.

It was with grim determination that he spent the remainder of the day seeing to the installation of an office in one of the downstairs rooms and getting his driver to bring his items of clothing from his own apartment to the house.

By four-fifteen he was ready and waiting for her arrival back home. The fact that she had no idea that he had chosen that day to move in, indeed had probably thought that he had dismissed the idea, having given her three days' reprieve during which nothing had been said on the subject, did not unduly bother him. He had, in fact, elected that particular day because he knew that Nicola would be having tea with one of her friends from school. It would leave him time to placate Julia without the presence of his daughter.

He had obtained a key for the house on the spurious excuse that as Nicola's father he had a right to have immediate access to her should the need arise, and had squashed every objection provided with a flat refusal to discuss the issue. Had behaved, in fact, in a manner that had infuriated Julia and disgusted himself, but his single-mindedness in getting what he wanted had been too great a spur.

He was in the sitting room, waiting, when he heard the sound of the key in the front door.

Very calmly he walked to the sitting-room door and lazily leaned against the door frame, arms folded, watching as Julia bustled in, head bent as she tried to prevent the stack of books in her hands from crashing to the floor as she fumbled to stuff the key back into her handbag.

'Need help?' he drawled from where he was standing, observing, and predictably the stack of exercise books fell to the ground in a tangled heap.

Julia's head shot up and she stared at the apparition in front of her, open-mouthed.

'What are you doing here?' The shock of seeing him when she had been thinking about him was surreal, and she blinked, wondering whether the powerful, dark vision in front of her was just a figment of her fevered imagination.

Riccardo pushed himself away from the door frame and strolled towards her, then he bent down at her feet and began collecting the books, stacking them into a haphazard pile that he held out for her.

When she continued to stare at him, flabbergasted and red-faced, he dumped the lot on the table and then stared back at her with his hands in his pockets.

'What are you *doing* here?' Julia repeated. Her voice was a few notches higher. 'And how did you get in?'

Riccardo dangled his key in front of her. 'I got a copy of the front-door key. Remember?'

Yes. She did. She snatched the key from him and dashed it onto the table alongside the books. 'To be used in emergencies only, you assured me!'

'Oh, yes. So I did. But this *is* an emergency.' He smiled very slowly at her. Julia had never managed to get accustomed to those smiles of his. They always seemed to go straight to the very heart of her, making her feel weak. She held on to the ledge of the table for support.

'Oh, it is, is it? And *where exactly* is the emergency?' Her brain began functioning again and she stood upright, glowering. 'I don't see any fire, or floods.'

'Well, perhaps emergency is the wrong word. Let's just say I needed to get in.'

'For what? Nicola is at her friend's house and won't be back until six.'

'I know.'

'You know.'

'Which, actually, is why I chose to come now. I've moved in.'

The three little words hung in the air between them as Julia attempted to absorb the full impact of them. 'You can't have,' she finally told him shakily. 'I told you that it was a ludicrous idea. I told you that under no circumstances would I entertain the thought of you moving into this house. If you recall, I said that you could see Nicola whenever you wanted but that this house was out of bounds as far as you were concerned!'

'Yes, so you did. But I moved in anyway.' He smiled again, unruffled. Had she any idea how edible she looked standing there, flustered, stammering and overwhelmed? He wanted to kiss her protesting mouth, devour her outburst with his tongue. 'Care to see where I've installed my office?' He began walking towards the seldom-used dining room, as much to put some distance between them as anything else. Harbouring erotic thoughts about her wasn't going to get him anywhere, and if her eyes happened to drift downwards she would probably run screaming through the front door.

'Your office?' she shrieked from behind him, flouncing in his wake. 'Your office? You already *have* an office! It's in the City! You go there every day to work!'

'Correction,' he called out, without looking around, 'I own the building in which my office happens to be located. And now you could say I have two.' He stood in front of the dining room, waiting for her to catch up, and, when she did, stood back so that she could view the efforts of the dozen or so men who had worked through lunch under his instructions to have the room up and running before mid-afternoon.

'I'm dreaming,' Julia said as she took in the dining-room table, now converted into a desk, on which rested his computer, phone, fax machine, and several files. 'This is all a dream. In a minute, I'll wake up.'

'No dream. But I could pinch you if you like.'

'Why?'

'I told you why.'

'Look at me,' Julia said, spreading her arms wide to indicate her very suitable outfit of deep-grey skirt, white blouse and matching jacket. She had maintained her working wardrobe, the only difference to her appearance being her hair and the visibility now of her luminous grey eyes. 'Do I look like an immoral woman setting a bad example for a child?'

This wasn't about how she looked, Riccardo thought in a blinding flash, or about any ridiculous idea that her dress code would somehow be unsuitable to be seen by a child; this was about him. *She* was why he had felt the compulsion to move in, why he had been given no choice in the matter. He turned away as a dark flush spread along his cheekbones.

'I've taken one of the guest rooms. And now, I've got work to do,' he said abruptly.

'We're not finished discussing this!' Julia snapped, walking straight into his line of vision so that he had to look at her.

'You might not be finished discussing this,' Riccardo said, sitting at one of the chairs and switching on his computer, 'but I am.'

'And where am *I* supposed to do my marking?' she demanded, walking to where he was seated with his face averted and staring down at him, hands on her hips. 'I don't like marking in the kitchen because it means having to clear it all away for tea, and, besides, that's where Nicola's accustomed to doing her drawing!'

'You can share the table with me,' he told her, busily clicking on icons on the computer so that he could access his work.

So much for discussion, Julia thought as she watched him frown at whatever it was he was viewing on the screen in front of him. Autocratic did not begin to cover his attitude. Nor did the word hopeless begin to cover hers. Because looking at him surreptitiously as he sat there, unaware of her existence, she was filled with a stupid feeling of elation. He had moved in lock, stock and barrel without bothering to consult her first, had laid down his orders like a master stating a decree, and instead of feeling enraged and resentful she felt excited and idiotically completed. Julia ground her teeth together in self-disgust and went out to the hall, gathering all the exercise books in her arms.

'Don't think we're finished with this one,' she informed him, sitting at the dining-room table and making a deal of spreading the books in front of her.

Riccardo grunted something in response but didn't look at her.

'Because I'm not. I just haven't got the time to say what I want to say if I'm to get these marked before I have to go and fetch Nicola.'

Another grunt. Riccardo looked at her from under his lashes, his eyes raking over her downbent head as she busily scanned the page in front of her, one hand poised with a red pen for marking. He had no idea what was on the computer screen in front of him. E-mails by the dozen. He would have to read them later. He couldn't think straight with her just within touching distance.

After a while, he abandoned the effort and idly picked up one of the exercise books lying between them and began reading. His lips began to twitch. When he gave a hoot of laughter Julia looked up from what she was doing and frowned.

'I thought you were supposed to be working,' she said crushingly, speaking to the top of his head, as the rest was hidden behind the exercise book.

'I was,' Riccardo said, lowering the book so that he

could look at her over the top of it. 'But this is a lot more interesting.

'It was snowing outside when suddenly the baby was born. It looks very big, said the mum. It had a green face and three legs because in fact it was a monster.

'What are you teaching these poor children?' he asked, pushing back the chair and stretching his legs onto the table-top.

'Do you mind removing your feet from the table? I always tell Nicola that table-tops are not for sitting on or standing up on.'

'Do many of your pupils suffer from nightmares?' Riccardo asked idly.

'It was a project on adventures,' Julia said, glancing over to him and feeling a churning feeling in her stomach as he gazed back at her, with his hands behind his head. It was sinful that a man could be so good-looking, she thought. If he were plain and uninspiring she would never have found herself in this situation. 'Rory has a very active imagination and he seems to be fixated with monsters.'

And who are you fixated with? he wanted to know. Roger? The mystery stockbroker with the sweaty palms? She must be keen on him or else she would never have accepted his phone number. That deduction had been playing on his mind and he could not get rid of it. He knew her. If the man's advances had been unwelcome she would have put on that cool, closed expression of hers and politely turned him away. It was a good thing that he had decided to move in here, he thought restlessly. He could keep an eye on her. Make sure she didn't bring home strange men for his daughter to meet. In fact, a little voice whispered, make sure she didn't bring home *any* men at all.

'What?' he asked as he realised that she was saying something to him, and Julia frowned.

'I said, could I please have the exercise book back. I want to mark it.'

Riccardo scooted it towards her and reclined back in the chair, staring at the tips of his shoes. 'What are we going to do about dinner?'

'Ah, yes.' Julia stood up and walked across to the bay window, where she perched on the sill. 'Another reason why this arrangement is not going to work out. I have got neither the time nor the inclination to start preparing meals for you on those days you happen to be around...'

'I'll be around a lot,' Riccardo drawled. 'Naturally, I shall still attend meetings during the day, but I plan on working a lot from here and also spending a lot of my evenings here as well. Getting to know Nicola better.' He looked down, slightly embarrassed by the patent shortcomings of this statement.

'As well as making sure that I don't set a bad example,' Julia said shortly.

'You can understand my feelings. I won't have you bringing strange men back to this house.'

Julia looked around her for a bit of heavenly assistance. How was she ever going to withstand the impact of this man on her if he intended to be around all the time, getting under her skin? And what gave him the right to keep an eye on her? It was an insult. He didn't trust her with Nicola and she could have told him that she had been doing a very good job of it and since Caroline and Martin were no longer around. She had been diligent, compassionate, understanding. Had choked back her own feelings of loss at the death of her brother, so as to maintain the semblance of strength that Nicola had so desperately needed. Did he really think that a change of appearance was going to alter her personality?

It felt good for her anger to begin surfacing. Better than the stupid feeling of contentment that had treacherously slipped over her as she had sat marking exercise books, feeling his masculine presence wafting across to her, pushing her to do something really pathetic, like sidle over to him and curl up on his lap, let him take her against all reason.

'I have no intention of bringing *strange men* back to this house!'

'What about the stockbroker? He's hardly a lifelong friend of the family!'

'There's nothing strange about Roger,' Julia retorted. 'In fact, you're a thousand times stranger than he is!'

'Ah, so another of your sissy men. Why bother? You will just go off him eventually when you discover how deeply boring he is.' Riccardo could hear the biting jealousy in his voice and flinched. 'In the meanwhile, I forbid you to bring him here.'

'You forbid? *You* forbid *me* to bring a friend back to this house?'

'Not a friend, a *man*.' Every pore in his body was revolting against the irony of the stance he was now adopting. He, a man who had always professed to abhor possessiveness in people, who had always detested when any of his girlfriends had tried to pin him down. Here he was, doing his damnedest to pin this woman down as tightly as he could. She had admitted to using him, had waltzed into his life and exercised the sort of control no other woman had ever dared to. He should be removing himself as far from her as possible.

'Are you jealous?' Julia asked hesitantly, and he banged his fist on the table.

'Jealous? Me? I have never been jealous of anyone in my life!' He stood up and began prowling around the room, as if he could no longer contain the energy coursing through his veins. 'Do I look like the type of man who is ever jealous?' he demanded, stopping in front of her. 'Do I?'

'Weren't you jealous of Martin?'

'I was never jealous of your brother!' Riccardo snarled. 'Furious, yes. He had stolen what was mine! But jealous, never.'

'Stolen what was yours?'

'Perhaps I used the wrong expression,' he rasped irritably as she raised her eyebrows in disbelief of the sentiment he had unwittingly expressed.

'You must have loved her very much,' Julia said quietly. Just saying it aloud sent a stab of pain to her heart and it took all her strength not to wilt in the face of the big man towering over her, not to let him see how much it pained her to think of him loving another woman, hurting when she walked away from him, maybe even nursing that hurt through the years as woman after woman failed to live up to his original blonde.

'Why do you say that?'

'Because of your possessiveness towards her, because of the anger you still feel after all this time at the thought of Martin.'

'I am Italian. She was my wife. Of course I was possessive. It would have been unnatural not to be. And I am angry with her and with your brother for concealing my own child from me, for taking that decision into their hands and playing God! As for loving Caroline, yes, of course I loved her. I married her! I happen to be a man who takes the vows of marriage very seriously. I would never have proposed if I had not loved her. Or thought that I did.'

Julia's heart gave a little lurch at that qualifying remark and she feverishly reminded herself that even if he no longer loved his ex-wife, was no longer driven by the need to try and replace what he had lost by cultivating a line of girlfriends more or less in her mould, then it still meant nothing. Because he didn't love *her*.

She felt her eyes glaze over as she concentrated on trying to read what was scrawled on the paper in front of her.

'Are you not going to ask me what I mean by that?'

'I told you, I have to get these books marked before I pick up Nicola.' She carefully circled a grammatical error to prove to him that she was already focusing on something else.

'I thought you prided yourself on liking New Man?' Riccardo said. He had never discussed his marriage or its collapse with anyone before. Not even with his family. His only response to them had been a curt withdrawal and a quelling observation that the past was another country, and, as such, beyond discussion. The few girlfriends who had expressed an interest had not even gotten that far. He had simply looked at them with a shuttered expression and changed the subject, leaving them in no doubt that his private life was forbidden territory.

It irked him now to think that he was willing to talk to Julia—in fact, driven to talk to her—about his marriage.

Julia looked up from what she was doing. 'Are you trying to tell me that you've suddenly become a new man, Riccardo?' She couldn't stop herself from grinning at the incongruity of the image presented, of Riccardo, the epitome of everything potently and exclusively male, shedding tears, discussing feelings and tinkering with healthy-eating recipe books. 'Does this mean that you intend to share the cooking, the cleaning and the ironing with me?'

'Ah, so I take it you are no longer going to fight me on my decision to move in here with you and Nicola.' He shot her a smile of barely concealed triumph. 'Naturally, I shall share the cooking. As for the rest, I intend to employ someone to take over the irritating little chores of cleaning and ironing.'

'Just as I expected,' Julia said feebly. 'You've been here two minutes and already you're laying down laws.'

'In fact, I could probably get someone in to do the cooking as well,' he announced. 'I am sure Pierre would not object.'

'Pierre?'

'My chef.'

'You have a chef?' Julia had the giddy feeling that she was being swept along by a series of rapid decisions and all she could do was cling to the coat tails of the conversation in a desperate attempt to hang on.

'He cooks for me when I need him. Of course, I pay him handsomely for his efforts.'

'Of course,' Julia said drily. 'An interesting variation on the new man. Not so much cooking, cleaning and ironing, as hiring the appropriate staff. I'm not so sure that that approach will ever get you accepted at the new-man club.'

He grinned at her and she reluctantly grinned back, feeling the shaky ground shift under her feet as she was held captive by his lazy, pervasive charm.

'But I have no intention of allowing you to lay down laws and regulations,' she said sternly, trying not to break into another grin as he did a poor show of looking chastened.

'Just doing the best I can to help the household run smoothly. I don't want to be a nuisance.'

'And don't put on that pious face. It doesn't work with me.'

'No, of course not.' He lowered his eyes, exultant at his victory. Of course, he would have stayed even if she had packed his bags and thrown them out onto the drive. And from his advantageous position he would make sure that the stockbroker wimp didn't set foot under the roof. If Julia thought that she was going to try those new-found wings then she was sorely mistaken. He felt absolutely no shame or guilt in his intention to keep her movements firmly under check, and as his thought clarified he knew why. Because he still wanted her. She had backed away from him, she had taken the phone number of another man, but he still wanted her, and have her he would.

Like it or not, the woman pulsed in his veins like his own life blood. He felt a shadowy unease when he tried to figure out why, and shoved the thought to one side.

She's a challenge, he decided to himself, and challenges, in his eyes, were to be met. He wanted to feel her soft and yielding against him, wanted her to think of no other man but him, he wanted to dominate her thoughts and her dreams.

But to do so he would have to fit in with her. That in itself, he thought wryly, would be a challenge, taking into account his personality.

'I shall prepare something for us to eat when you go to fetch Nicola,' he said magnanimously, and she threw him a sceptical look.

'What?'

'There is no need for you to look so dubious, Julia,' he said with a slow smile. 'I spent my childhood surrounded by great cooks. Cooking is in my blood.'

'And you have a way of transferring all this wonderful knowledge from your blood onto a plate, have you?'

'Leave it to me. In fact, you stay here and carry on with your marking and I shall make inroads into a meal.' He strolled over to his computer and switched it off. E-mails would just have to wait until later.

How she had managed to finish doing any work at all, Julia thought later as she headed off to collect Nicola, was a miracle. Even though he was no longer in the room with her, just knowing that he was in the kitchen was enough to rattle her.

But she would not let him get to her, she decided firmly. She would maintain a detached and healthy distance. She certainly would not allow him to undermine her social life.

She thought of Roger and wondered what she would do if he called, because she had certainly no intention of calling him. Would she go on a date? The thought of doing that was not inviting, but she realised that giving in to the alternative of staying at home and falling into any kind of routine with Riccardo was just downright dangerous.

By the time she arrived back at the house she had explained to Nicola that her father had moved in, which had met with an excited, childish yelp. And as far as bonding went, she could see that his presence did have certain advantages. It would increase their familiarity with one another. She watched as he drew pictures with her and left him to have her shower sitting on the sofa with the cartoon channel switched on.

In no time at all, Riccardo and Nicola would have forged the necessary bond that would give them the strength to fly away together.

And then what? Julia thought as she slipped into a pair of faded jeans and one of her small white ribbed tops. He would vanish with his daughter, only keeping in touch occasionally so that Nicola and she could maintain links. He would no longer have any need to live under her roof, to keep his eye on her, as he seemed to think necessary. She would have to set in motion some kind of life that could support her just to fill the inevitable gaping void he would leave behind.

She settled Nicola, who had worked herself up into a state of excitement as she contemplated the long list of thrilling activities that would now begin with Riccardo living under the same roof, and then walked slowly down to the kitchen.

She paused in the doorway for a few seconds to watch him unobserved as he stirred something in a frying pan and then lifted the lid on a saucepan.

'Smells good,' Julia said, stepping into the kitchen, and he turned around to look at her. 'What is it?' She could feel his presence drugging her.

'An old Italian recipe handed down through the ages,' Riccardo drawled, his eyes covertly flicking over her, taking in the skimpy little top that left very little to the imagination while still managing to send it rocketing into fifth gear. 'I used everything I could lay my hands on in the fridge and added a delicate mixture of herbs and spices. Sit.' He poured her a glass of white wine and Julia obediently sat at the kitchen table, trying not to over-relish the sheer pleasure of being waited on by him. How the hell did he manage to look so sexy in front of a cooker? He had rolled up the sleeves of his shirt, displaying his muscled forearms, and the slight sheen of perspiration on his face only added to his raw sex appeal. Her nerves began to jump and she hastily swallowed a mouthful of wine.

'Nicola's very excited about your moving in,' she said as he ladled food into serving dishes and began bringing them to the table.

'I like to think so. She asked if she could call me Dad. She told me that all her friends have dads and that she has always dreamed of hers. Of me,' he said proudly, before resuming his clipped voice. 'At least,' he huffed, to cover the uneven softening in his voice when he had spoken about his daughter, 'one of you is.' He twirled spaghetti around a long fork and slid a generous helping onto her plate. Even that slight action delineated the muscles in his forearms. Relaxing was going to be a major feat in his presence. 'Now dig in,' he commanded, waiting so that he could hear her verdict.

'Very good.' Their eyes met and he smiled with satisfaction.

'Did I not tell you that cooking is in my blood?'

'I didn't know whether to believe you or not. You don't strike me as a very domesticated figure.'

'Perhaps I never met the right woman who could domesticate me,' he drawled, his black eyes watching her steadily as he twirled some spaghetti around his fork.

'Not even Caroline?' She had been itching to bring up the subject of his ex-wife and get him to explain his mysterious insinuation that he had only thought he had been in love with her.

'I wondered when you would get back to that,' Riccardo said.

'I'm just making conversation, Riccardo. If you don't want to talk about it, then don't. It's all the same to me.'

'Caroline never managed to domesticate me, no. I look back now, and perhaps I can say in all honesty that she tried. Tried and failed.' He thought of his ex-wife and realised that for the first time he was glad that she had found happiness with another man. She had deserved it. 'I wasn't open to making sacrifices,' he murmured, more to himself than to his rapt audience, 'and, of course, making sacrifices is what a good marriage is all about. I found her twittering around me irritating after a while. I also found it hard to conceal my irritation.'

'Which is why she became more and more withdrawn,' Julia pointed out softly.

'Yes, she did. And the more withdrawn she became, the more irritated and impatient I became. In the end, it was a vicious circle. We barely spoke, and when we did we never seemed to get anywhere with the conversations.' He shrugged and sighed. 'Two people who started out with the best of intentions and just came unstuck somewhere along the way. But that was no reason for her to keep Nicola a secret from me.'

'No, no, it wasn't,' Julia agreed, and he shot her a brooding look from under his lashes.

'You were in on the scheme. How can you sit there and calmly agree with me?'

'I was not *in on the scheme*,' Julia retorted, closing her fork and spoon on her empty plate and taking a sip of wine. 'You seem to think that I was living here and party to every little decision Caroline and Martin made. I wasn't. I was renting my own flat on the other side of town and, whilst I didn't agree with their decision to keep you in the dark about your daughter, I didn't feel there was much that I could do, and I suppose I had my own life to think about.'

'You had no opinions on me?'

'I didn't *know* you, Riccardo! I only knew you from what Caroline told me and I was too busy with my own life to become involved in what was going on in my brother's! When they died...' Julia's voice faltered '...I realised that I had to make a decision and I decided to do what I had always thought they should have done. I decided to get in touch with you.'

'And are you pleased that you did?'

Julia picked up the faintest, fleeting shadow of innuendo

in his question. He was referring to far more than whether she was pleased that Nicola now had contact with her real father. Or so she imagined.

He toyed with some pasta on his fork and looked at her with a darkly inscrutable expression.

'Of course I am,' she answered jumpily. 'Nicola deserves to know you and she always has, even if she was denied the chance. I can see that you'll make a wonderful father. You're kind and thoughtful with her, and caring...' Her words were drying up in her throat as he continued to watch her, his dark eyes not once straying from her face, which was getting pinker by the minute.

'And if we leave Nicola out of the equation,' he said softly, 'are you still pleased that you contacted me?'

'Well...I...it's always nice to get to know different people...' Julia said weakly.

'Because I am.'

'You are?' She could only give in to her fascinated trance.

'I am. When we first met, I told you that you weren't my type of woman. I was wrong. You are very much my type of woman.' He swallowed a mouthful of wine as he appraised her flustered face. 'I made love to you once and I intend to make love to you again. Because I still want you and that's why your Roger stockbroker will not be calling you and neither will you be calling him.' His voice was perfectly calm. Calm and reasonable, for all the world as though they were discussing the weather. 'Your body is for my enjoyment only.'

'For your enjoyment!' Julia gasped, ashamed to admit even to herself that his Italian possessiveness had turned her body to water and set in motion a thousand sweetly

seductive images in her head. 'What we did was a mistake, Riccardo!' she said in a shaky voice. 'And I'm not after a casual affair!'

'Then tell me what you *are* after.'

CHAPTER NINE

JULIA stared at him, pinned to the chair by his dark, brooding gaze. This was a terrible mistake, but then she had known that it would be. They couldn't exist under the same roof, sharing meals and conversations, while he kept her movements under check and began a slow process of seduction. She was too weak when it came to dealing with him. She just wanted too much, much more than he was capable of giving, and surrendering to their mutual lust was not a good enough reason for her to yield.

But she could feel her body burning under his stare, quivering with desire.

'We should clear up,' she mumbled, pushing back her chair and stumbling to her feet. Her hair fell over her eyes and she feverishly brushed it away then picked up her dirty crockery and headed for the sink, making sure not to look at him.

So much for tactics, Riccardo thought, following her every movement across the kitchen and breathing in her discomfort. So much for the subtlety of the master seducer. He had barged right in like a bull in a china shop and left her dithering and withdrawing at a rate of knots.

But God, he couldn't stop himself! She made him behave like a schoolboy.

He swiftly cleared the remainder of the table, while she huddled protectively by the sink, washing dishes with her head lowered; then he picked up a tea towel and began drying.

The atmosphere between them was crackling with tension.

'Have you got around to telling your mother about my moving in?' Riccardo asked, and Julia looked at him with troubled eyes.

'What?'

'Your mother. Have you told her that I have moved in?'

'No. Ah, I didn't…I haven't had the opportunity as yet.' She returned to the fork in her hand, washing it more carefully than was required. She could smell the clean, tangy, masculine scent of him, filling her nostrils, and she edged a little away from his arm next to hers.

'How do you think she will react? It never occurred to me that mothers might be a bit protective about their daughters living with a man.'

'You're Nicola's father; it's an unusual situation but Riccardo, I don't think this situation…can…is going to work out. I…'

'Why not?'

'Because…' Her voice trailed away into silence and she could feel his eyes on her, running over her flustered face and along her body.

'Because I have told you that I still want you?' Riccardo asked silkily, abandoning all his efforts to put her at her ease and not charge in. He wanted her to admit her attraction to him. It wasn't enough seeing it in her eyes. He wanted to hear it as well, wanted her to break down and confess that she couldn't resist him. He wanted her to come to him and the only way that was going to happen was if she was truthful, with herself and him. 'Would you rather that I had not said anything? Even though you must have felt it, must have seen it in my eyes whenever I looked at you.' He could feel himself getting hot under his collar as she clung to her stubborn silence. Dammit! This was taking

English reticence too far! 'And you're going to have to deal with this because I'm here now and I won't be going away.'

'You'll go away if I tell you to!' Julia bit out, her grey eyes flashing as they met hers. 'This is *my* house, in case you've forgotten!'

'Your house in which *my* daughter lives!' He knew that it was a low trick, bringing Nicola into the equation whenever he needed a winning card, but not all things in life were fair and playing by the book had never been one of his strong points. 'If it had not been for you, your brother and my ex-wife, this situation would never have arisen! Like it or not, you will just have to accept some of the responsibility for my being here in the first place!' A more convoluted argument it would have been hard to find, but he stood his ground, challenging her with a hard, unyielding stare.

'I won't tolerate you being here if you're going to make things awkward for me,' Julia told him unsteadily. She slipped off the daffodil-yellow washing-up gloves and draped them over the side of the sink, then she dried her hands on the small towel on the counter and sidled away from him, still watching him from under her lashes as though afraid that he might strike unexpectedly.

'In other words,' Riccardo mocked, turning around to look at her and folding his arms across his broad chest, 'I should just go along with the pretence that we're no more than, what...acquaintances? Two people who happen to be accidentally living under the same roof because of a third party? Tell me, do we converse at all or should I abide by strict guidelines that I never get too personal?' There was biting sarcasm in his voice that made Julia cringe.

'Of course we can be polite to one another—'

'Polite!' He gave a crack of hard laughter and walked towards her. 'We made love and yet you expect us both to behave like polite strangers when we're in each other's presence?'

'I…I wish you wouldn't keep bringing that up,' Julia stammered.

'There are a lot of things you seem to wish.' He stopped in front of her. It took supreme will-power to fight down his natural urge to say what needed to be said and hang the consequences. 'Look,' he sighed and raked his long fingers through his hair, then stuck his hands in his pockets, 'we're standing here arguing. I do not want to argue with you. Why don't I make us both a cup of coffee and we can go into the sitting room and discuss this like two adults?'

'You mean you're prepared to stop bullying me?'

'Is that what you think I'm doing?'

Julia hated herself for melting whenever he came close to her, whenever he spoke, whenever he so much as glanced in her direction. How could she be rational and logical when he made her feel as if she was walking along the edge of a cliff in a strong wind?

'Isn't it?' Julia asked, sticking her chin out and refusing to go weak-kneed.

'I don't bully,' Riccardo said, briefly looking away.

'No, you just carry on shouting until you get your own way.'

'Now you make me sound like a toddler. Throwing a temper tantrum if he doesn't get some sweets.' His voice was so disarmingly rueful that Julia felt herself beginning to smile, only to dimly remember the cause of their argument.

He could move from rage to charm, from aggression to humour so seamlessly that he never failed to take her by surprise. Was that how she had so carelessly managed to fall in love with him? Because her defences couldn't withstand the complexity of his personality? Every other man she had ever met seemed one-dimensional in comparison.

'Now, you go and wait for me in the sitting room and I shall bring some coffee in. And you have my word that I won't raise my voice or bully you. Deal?'

'Why do I trust you even less when you're being nice, Riccardo?'

'Because you're suspicious.' He held his hands up in mock-surrender. 'I will be as good as gold.'

Julia headed for the sitting room, vaguely aware that she had somehow been manoeuvred, and then sat on the sofa, her legs curled up beneath her. God, he might drive her crazy, scare the hell out of her when she thought of the damage he could do to her heart, but every pore in her body felt alive when he was around. It just wasn't fair!

He came in a few minutes later, carrying a circular tray on which were two cups, the glass jug of percolated coffee and a small jug of milk. 'I waited tables when I was at university to earn some money,' he said, resting the tray on the table and sitting on the sofa. 'Are you impressed?'

'*You waited tables?* I'm not impressed, Riccardo, I'm surprised,' Julia said, diverted by this revelation. She watched as he poured her a cup of coffee and handed the cup to her.

He shot her a gleaming look over his shoulder as he leaned to pour himself a cup. 'Did you imagine that I would never do anything so menial as waiting tables?'

'I imagined that you would not have had to. Caroline said that—'

'I came from a lot of money? You and my ex-wife seem to have had quite a lot of conversations about me.'

'I guess there was a lot of stuff she needed to get off her chest.' Julia shrugged and hoped that this would not lead to another surge of anger over his ex-wife's dubious politics concerning their daughter, but he seemed relaxed.

'My family is very wealthy; I would be the first to admit it.' He sat back and stretched out his legs. 'But I never felt that I had the right to use their wealth when I was perfectly capable of supporting myself. I did a number of jobs when I was at university, including bartending and holiday work at a building company. Now, that is what I would call hard work. Lifting bags of cement and heaving bricks.'

Julia imagined him bare-backed under the summer sun, body glistening with sweat as he heaved bricks, and her cheeks pinkened at the violently erotic image her mind conjured up. He would have been the sort of workman that women paused to wolf-whistle rather than the other way around!

'I worked my way through university as well,' she admitted. 'Although that was largely from necessity.'

'What did you do?' There seemed no end to his curiosity. He wanted to find out everything he could about this woman, every little detail of her life.

'I worked at the check-out tills at the supermarket in the evenings. It was fun. The people were a good laugh. And I worked in shops.' She smiled at the memory and sipped her coffee.

'So we have more in common than you admit,' Riccardo murmured and he sensed her tense, but he would just have to break through that tension. Either that or remain politely distant until the time came for him to leave with his daughter. And he was not going to remain politely distant.

'We should be able to share this house quite amicably,' he continued.

'You know why we can't, Riccardo.'

'I know why we might not be able to...'

'It's the same thing.' Julia rested her cup on the table

and drew her knees up, circling them with her arms as she looked at him.

'It is very far from being the same thing,' he told her conversationally. 'If I thought we couldn't share this house because our personalities were incompatible then I would never have moved in. But I don't. The reason we might not be able to share this house is because I am honest about the way I feel, while you persist in holding on to a lie.' His voice was quite calm, as were the dark eyes resting on her flushed face. Persuasively calm.

'Why do you have to insist on reducing everything to a personal level?' Julia pleaded.

'Because, whether you want to admit it or not, the personal level exists between us. I can feel it throbbing in the air whenever we're in the same room, I can feel it down the end of the line whenever you're on the phone! Why pretend otherwise?' When she didn't answer he shook his head impatiently. 'You never answered my question.'

'What question?'

'The one I asked you earlier. You told me that you weren't after a casual affair. So what *are* you after, Julia? Love, marriage and fireworks? Romance with all the frills and a happy-ever-after ending?' His mouth twisted cynically and Julia blinked rapidly as tears tried to push their way through from under her eyelids.

This was why they had to be polite to one another! Because every time feelings entered the equation a Pandora's box was opened and they came up against the same, immovable brick wall.

'I thought you were immune to such dreams?' he pressed on ruthlessly. 'I thought you had rebelled against your mother's nagging for you to settle down, have two children and spend the rest of your life playing the housewife.'

'I'm just not interested in having a casual affair.' Her

mouth was set in a stubborn line and she began to stand up, to run away from the conversation, but his hand descended on her wrist, forcing her to remain where she was.

'You've had affairs in the past, haven't you? You're not a virgin!'

'I haven't *had affairs* in the past! You make it sound as though I've led a life of debauchery! I had a couple of boyfriends, yes, but that's it!'

'So why is it so different this time?' he asked, jerking her towards him, his eyes grim.

Because I'm in love with you, Julia wanted to throw at him. Because I can't just have uninvolved *fun* with you! I want too much.

'Maybe I'm just getting older,' she said, her breath catching painfully in her throat. 'I don't want to waste any more time with someone who isn't meant for me. So it doesn't matter about physical attraction or about whether you want me or I want you. I might want you, Riccardo...' Saying it hurt but she had to, or else he would pursue her. Challenges for a man like Riccardo were fine, just provided none of them got away. If they did then he would chase them to the ends of the earth and back, but if she mentioned commitment and marriage he would back off. She looked at him without flinching. 'I just don't want what you have to offer.'

'Are you sure about that?' he murmured lazily. He began to gently caress the tender back of her wrist with his thumb and Julia's eyes widened.

'Very sure,' she replied hoarsely.

'How can you say that,' he chided softly, 'when you haven't sampled all I have to offer? It is very small-minded to reject something when you haven't first tried it.'

'I don't think...tha...that that refers to sexual experimentation,' Julia whispered. He was no longer holding her wrist, yet still her arm refused to move. It lay there, leaden and impassive, inviting him to run his forefinger from elbow to wrist, making her shiver.

He mesmerised her, and the devil knew it. She could hear it in his smoky voice and see it in the slow smile.

'You want a routine courtship and a white wedding,' he drawled softly, 'but take it from me, there's more to life than marriage. What we have is bigger than both of us...why fight it?' He shifted until he was close to her, then he very gently smoothed her legs flat so that she was lying on the sofa and staring up at his darkly sexy face.

'I miss your spectacles,' he murmured wryly. 'There is something very erotic about removing a woman's glasses.'

'You've done a lot of that in the past, have you?'

'Never,' he admitted, tantalising her senses with another of those lingering smiles. 'I pride myself on being open for new experiences.'

'And that's what I am, isn't it, Riccardo? A new experience.'

He halted the fight she wanted by putting his finger on her lips. Then he held both her hands and raised them to the back of the sofa so that she was stretched out for his hungry eyes.

They could argue until the cows came home, he thought as his body reared up in response to the sight of her, she could preach about right and wrong and should and shouldn't, but they were drawn to each other like magnets.

He lowered his head and kissed her. It was a lingering kiss and he traced her lips delicately with his tongue, explored the softness of her mouth until she was gasping.

Then he kissed her neck, nibbling the slender white column, letting their anticipation mount while his thoughts played with images of her nakedness, milky white against his copper skin.

'Riccardo...'

'Ssh, don't talk.' She wasn't wearing a bra. He knew that much, had spotted it as soon as she had appeared after her shower. The top was not transparent and she probably wasn't even aware of how lovingly it shaped the contours of her breasts. He teased her collarbone with his mouth and with a little groan Julia curled her fingers into his hair.

This shouldn't be happening! But the minute he touched her she was lost. She didn't just want him, she was burning up with it! She wanted to taste him, that sweetly addictive masculine taste that dragged her into a vortex of desire.

She gave a little squeak when his mouth moved down to her breasts and he began sucking her nipple through her clinging top, dampening it until the outline of her nipple was evident.

'No bra,' he murmured, lifting his gaze to her.

'I hardly ever wear one when I'm in the house,' Julia panted unsteadily.

'Keep it that way,' he laughed huskily and resumed his tender nibbling of her breast, saving himself for the moment when he could lift her top and view the real thing.

One hand stroked the line of her thigh. Jeans had to be the most frustrating item in a woman's wardrobe, he thought. Now if she had been wearing a skirt he could have felt her skin under his, felt every little shudder.

He gently lifted the top and groaned as he looked at her pert nipples, aroused and dark. He flicked his tongue over one and she shifted on the sofa, releasing little sighs of contentment that went straight to the core of him, making him want to take her right there and right now, without the preliminaries of foreplay.

'If you don't want this, tell me now,' he ordered roughly.

'You know I don't want it,' Julia moaned, but when he

raised his head she pulled him back down. 'I don't want it, but I need it. Make love to me, Riccardo.'

The sweetest words ever uttered. He stood up, watching her watching him, and undid his belt, letting it slither to the ground, then he unzipped his trousers and stepped out of them.

Julia had never found anything remotely fascinating about male strippers. In fact, on the one occasion she had gone with a gang of friends to see some perform at a club for a hen party she had found the sight of men removing their clothes positively comical.

But this was mind-blowingly erotic. She knew that he was looking at her, maybe amused by her intent gaze, maybe turned on by it, but she couldn't help herself. She watched as he removed his clothing and then carried on watching when he stood in front of her, unashamedly masculine and very obviously turned on.

'Now it's your turn,' he said, standing proudly male while she slowly stood up and began fumbling with the button on her jeans. She might have changed her image and polished her exterior, but her newly acquired outward shine certainly did not penetrate below skin level. She had never been watched by a man before, not like this, not knowing that his eyes were focused on her every movement, and her hands were slippery with nerves.

'I wish you wouldn't stand watching me like that, Riccardo,' she said shyly, and he grinned.

'OK. I'll sit.' He sat down and watched. Not much better from her self-conscious point of view.

But it was a sight he would not have missed for the world. So gauche, so unrehearsed, so utterly, utterly feminine with it. He had a stab of painful regret that he had not been the one to gently lead her out of her virginity. Her fingers were trembling and he wanted to pull her towards him and bury her against his chest.

She modestly stood, nude, before him, her arms crossed and he beckoned her to him with the crook of one finger.

'You are beautiful,' he murmured throatily, tucking her alongside him on the sprawling sofa. She needed tenderness, and he made love tenderly, rousing her with his tongue, with his hands, with his fingers, tracing the outline of her body, revelling in her pliancy and bringing her to the point of orgasm, only to thrust inside her with an explosion of fulfilment when neither of them could hold out any longer.

Julia lay against him, her head on his chest, listening to the rhythm of his heartbeat.

When she stirred he gently pushed her head back into its resting position.

'Now tell me what we just did was a mistake,' he said softly and Julia sighed.

'You know it was. It won't happen again.'

'A one-off?' he said, lazily content. 'Like the last time? We are irresistibly drawn to one another. Now is the time for you to admit it.'

His words flowed around her, confusing her. Was he right? Should she just acquiesce and go with the flow, then sort out the consequences when they arose?

It took her a few seconds to register the distant trilling of the telephone.

'Let it ring,' he commanded as she struggled up. 'We have to talk.'

'I can't let it ring. It might be Mum. It might be important.' And she didn't want to talk. Not yet. She didn't know what she could say to him. She needed time. She hastily slung on her jeans and pulled the top over her head, leaving him sprawling on the sofa.

The house felt cold as she hurried through it, desperate to reach the phone before it wakened Nicola. Unlikely, but a possibility and one Julia could heartily do without.

'I was just about to ring off.'

'Who is it?' Julia was still breathing quickly from her race through the house. She had not buttoned the top of her jeans and she cradled the receiver between her head and her neck while she fumbled with them.

'Don't you recognise my voice?' There was an amused laugh down the end of the phone. 'So much for my unforgettable impact on the opposite sex.'

'Roger!'

'I've been thinking about you since the party, Julia. Would you like to come out with me? Movies? Theatre? A bite to eat afterwards?'

'Roger…I…'

She glanced furtively over her shoulder, half expecting to see Riccardo lounging indolently in the doorway. She had just had the most beautiful, meaningful experience in her entire life and he would be waiting for her, waiting to hear her tell him that she had caved in, was willing to have a fling with him and play at happy families until he decided the time was right to leave. He had spoken a lot about want and attraction but not one word had passed his lips, even in the depths of passion, about permanence or love or commitment.

Her jaw hardened. 'When were you thinking of going out?' she asked, blinking back tears and telling herself furiously that she was doing the right thing.

'Is tomorrow too soon?'

'Tomorrow's fine,' she heard herself say.

'Why don't you give me directions to your house? I can be there to pick you up at—'

'No! I mean, it would be a lot more convenient if I met you at…at wherever we're going.'

'OK.' He paused and she could hear him thinking down the end of the phone. 'There's an excellent Italian…'

'Not Italian. I'm…I don't care for Italian food.'

'How about French, then?' He sounded mildly surprised and Julia wondered whether he was cursing himself for arranging a date with a woman who sounded bizarre down the telephone.

'French is fine.' Julia closed her eyes and breathed deeply. 'What's it called and how do I get there?'

He gave her detailed directions, getting her to repeat them so that he could make sure that she knew where she would be going and then she said, 'I'll meet you there about seven-forty-five. Is that all right?'

'Better than all right. See you tomorrow.'

Julia walked slowly back to the sitting room to find Riccardo semi-dressed, with his trousers on, standing by the window, waiting.

'Important phone call?' he queried laconically, testing the water, but he knew, with a knot of anger and desperation in his gut, that he had lost her. She had that closed look on her face that spoke volumes. How? *How, dammit?* He wanted to break things, but he remained where he was, rigidly poised, looking at her.

Julia shrugged. 'I'm going to bed now.'

'We have to talk,' he grated and she gazed at him distantly.

'What about?'

'About us.'

'There *is* no us, Riccardo. Yes, we're attracted to one another, but there's no us and I'm not willing to have a fling.'

'And you've had time to make your mind up about that in the time it took for you to answer the telephone?'

Julia bravely met his eyes. God, how easily she could move over to him, run her hands over the hard, muscled chest and lift her mouth to his.

'That's right.'

'Why don't you stop hovering by the door and step inside the room?' He knew that if she did she would come to him, but he realised, suddenly, that it would be an empty victory and he flushed darkly. 'No, forget I said that,' he told her roughly. His pride kicked into gear. She had turned him down. Twice. No more. He was finished running behind her. Women were a dime a dozen, he thought viciously. He didn't need to pursue this one, whatever she did for him and however much of a challenge she was.

Julia looked at him hesitantly until he said coldly, 'I get the message loud and clear, Julia. So why don't you go to bed and we'll both be adult about this and pretend that nothing ever happened?' His mouth twisted cynically as he turned away to stare out of the window, his back to her.

It's for the best, Julia thought as she headed up to her bedroom. So why did she feel so hollow? Tomorrow she would begin the dating game. She would be going out with a perfectly nice man, a nice, *predictable* man who did not swing from one mood to the next in a matter of seconds. And if Roger wasn't the man for her then there would be another, and another, until she found one.

The following morning she awoke at her usual time to find that Riccardo had already left for work. His car was not in the drive and the half-empty cup of coffee on the kitchen counter showed that he had been up and out long before seven-thirty, which was when she and Nicola had come downstairs.

At lunchtime, still feeling peculiarly empty inside, Julia

called him at the office and was surprised when she was put through to him.

'I just want to find out whether you'll be in tonight,' she said, playing with the cord of the phone and talking quietly into the receiver because the staff room was full, with most of the teachers choosing to have their lunch at their desks.

'Why?'

'Because I'm going out tonight and I want to know whether I should ask Mum over to babysit.' In fact, she would have to get in touch with her mother later that day and explain the arrangement of Riccardo living in the house. At least she would be able to say, with her hand on her heart, that there was absolutely nothing going on between them, that Nicola now knew who he really was and so any so-called pretend relationship had ceased. The proof of that would be the presence of another man on the scene.

'I'll be home. What time are you leaving?'

'Around seven.'

'I'll be back.'

And that was the end of the conversation. She had demanded politeness from him and she had got exactly what she had wanted. His voice had been coolly courteous and Julia knew that his behaviour, when she saw him, would be as well.

She spent the remainder of the day at school operating on automatic, teaching her classes without really being aware of what was going on around her. She collected Nicola from kindergarten at a little after three-thirty and, instead of returning to the house, took her to the shopping mall for a treat and then to a fast-food restaurant, where Nicola chattered on relentlessly about everything under the sun, asking thousands of questions about her father which Julia had to answer as brightly and normally as she possibly could. How long had this child been waiting for the missing jigsaw piece of her father to be slotted in? Forever, it now seemed!

The house was in darkness when they returned at a little before six. So he wasn't back from work yet. Julia was unutterably relieved. She went through the motions, bathed Nicola, and then, with Nicola lying on her bed watching television, Julia got dressed, feeling all the while as though she were heading for her doom instead of preparing herself for a date, an exciting date, she told herself, with a good-looking, pleasant, eligible man.

And soon it would be the holidays. Nicola would be taken to Italy, without the necessity of needing a chaperon, and there she would see the sprawling family of which she was now a member and by whom she would be lovingly embraced.

But there would be no void because she would be dating, dating, dating.

She chose a sober but figure-hugging wool dress, short-sleeved with a scooped neckline, and the high heels, then she stood back and looked at herself. She looked glamorous rather than sexy and she was pleased with her reflection.

'Where are you going?' Nicola asked idly from the bed and Julia caught her eye in the mirror.

'Oh, just for a meal out, honey.'

'Who with?'

'A friend.'

'What friend?'

'Father Christmas.' Which evoked a response of thrilled excitement, and by the time they strolled downstairs Julia, at least, was smiling.

The sound of the key in the door and the sight of Riccardo entering almost eradicated the smile from her face, but she staunchly maintained it as their eyes met. He was in his working clothes, a dark, impeccably tailored suit that he wore with easy panache. Julia stifled the flutter of awareness as she looked at him and kept the remnants of the smile on her face.

'Nicola's eaten,' she said brightly, relieved when Nicola began describing their adventurous after-school activities of a shopping mall and burger.

'And I'll be back later,' she threw in, edging towards the door with her jacket slung over her arm and her bag in her hand.

'And where are you going?'

'I have the telephone number here and my mobile number.' She handed him a slip of paper and began opening the door, almost expecting him to try and stop her, but he was already turning away with uninterest, and his indifference sent an arrow of pain shooting through her.

'Have a good time.' With his back to her, he held out his hand for his daughter and Julia watched as the both of them left her standing by the door and headed towards the kitchen, with Nicola offering a cheery wave over her shoulder.

It already felt like the final goodbye.

CHAPTER TEN

THE French restaurant was just off the King's Road and, aside from its name discreetly etched on a gilt plaque on the wrought-iron railings, it could have been a private residence. It breathed good taste. Just the sort of restaurant to appeal to a stockbroker. Nothing flashy, nothing ostentatious. Very English.

Riccardo stood outside for a few moments, letting the cold air cool him down.

He had had no intention of being here. He had watched Julia leave the house and thought that he had been superbly self-contained. Indifferent even. He had turned his back on her, signalling that he did not give a damn where she was going or who she was going with.

He had put Nicola to sleep and had then proceeded to spend an hour in front of a stack of files, tapping his fountain pen on the table and frowning at the blur of writing in front of him.

Who had he been kidding?

He walked down the four concrete steps to the front of the restaurant and pushed open the door to find himself towering over a diminutive, smartly dressed waiter. His eyes quickly scanned the room which was loosely sectioned off into three eating areas, pausing when he saw the object of his search. She was sitting at a table in the corner, her face propped on the palm of her hand and looking at the man who was with her and who was talking animatedly about something.

'You have a reservation, sir?'

'No.' Riccardo did not even bother to look at the man who was giving him an ingratiatingly apologetic smile.

'Then I'm afraid—'

'I'm joining those two people over there.' He indicated Julia and her date with a jerk of his head.

'We were not told that there would be a third party.'

'Well, I'm telling you now.'

'I'm afraid...' The poor man's sentence remained unfinished as Riccardo began closing the distance between himself and Julia.

There was no lull in the low conversations as he strode past tables. The clientele were too well-bred to stare. He reached the table and only then did Julia look up, as he leaned forward and placed his hands firmly on the table-top, his body looming over them both intimidatingly.

'Riccardo!'

'Sir! I must ask you to leave at once. This is most unorthodox!'

'Bring me a chair,' was Riccardo's growling response and at the risk of causing an even greater stir, the waiter scurried off and returned with a chair.

'What are you d-doing here?' Julia stammered. 'Roger, this is...Riccardo. He's...he's babysitting for me. You haven't left Nicola in the house on her own, have you?'

'Your mother is with her.' He turned to Roger and bared his teeth into a menacing smile. 'Why don't you go, *old boy*? I'm taking over from here.'

'What's this all about, Julia?' enquired a confused Roger.

'Riccardo, please. *What are you doing here?*' One or two of the well-bred eyes were slanting in their direction and she sank into her chair.

'Yes, what the heck are you doing here? Julia, who *is* this man?'

'Why don't you tell him, Julia, *darling*?'

'I say, this simply isn't on.' Roger signalled to the waiter. 'This man is being a nuisance. Have him removed, please.'

The waiter hovered uncertainly behind Riccardo who ignored his presence. 'If you want me removed, *Roger*,' he drawled, pushing his face further forward so that the sheer force of his powerful personality became a thinly veiled threat, 'then I suggest you attempt to do so yourself.'

'I don't indulge in scraps.'

'Then why don't you either clear off or shut up?'

'Riccardo, this is *enough*! You're creating a scene and...and embarrassing everyone!' Julia licked her lips nervously and felt a tremor of wild awareness as his black eyes met hers with burning intensity.

He didn't answer. Instead he sat in the chair, leaned back with his eyes narrowed on Roger's blustering face and signalled a waiter over.

'A whisky.'

'This man is *not* joining us!'

'Julia...?' His black eyes swept over her flushed face, and in her moment of hesitation he smiled with tigerish satisfaction. 'Your date is at an end,' he said to Roger and Julia reddened as both men stared at her. Now was the time to firmly send Riccardo on his way, but she couldn't. She couldn't choose Roger because she knew with weary resignation that he was second best.

'Roger, perhaps you'd better leave. I'm very sorry, but if you don't we'll all probably end up being thrown out.'

'But—'

'But you heard the lady. Go.' His whisky had been brought to him and he sipped it, casually dismissing the hapless Roger, who stumbled to his feet, dropping the starched linen serviette on the table in front of him.

'Don't expect to hear from me again,' he told Julia, who

smiled weakly at him, and as soon as he had walked off she leaned forward and said in a low, angry voice,

'What do you mean by barging in here? How dare you interrupt my date?'

'Have you eaten?'

'Yes! No! We've had our starters. We *were* looking forward to enjoying our main course before you stormed in!' She looked at that dark, handsome face and felt a wave of irrational love wash over her, leaving her weak.

'Good. In that case, let's get out of here and go somewhere a little less...' he looked around him condescendingly '...stuffy.'

'I'm not going anywhere with you!'

'Oh, yes, you are.'

'Because you say so?'

'Because you want to.' He stood up while Julia gaped at his sheer arrogance, clumsily following suit when he tossed some notes on the table and beckoned their confused waiter across. 'This should cover the cost of the meal, with a very generous tip.'

'I do apologise...' Julia began, but he was already taking her arm in his vice-like grip and steering her towards the door. The well-bred clientele had given up on their etiquette and were now openly staring as she was ushered through the restaurant.

'You...*you*...*you caveman*!' she spluttered as soon as they were out of the restaurant.

'I'd rather be a caveman than a wimp. I didn't notice your knight in shining armour jumping in to your rescue.' He hailed a taxi and ensured that she was left no choice in the matter of climbing in by blocking the open door with his big, muscular body, then he slid in after her and gave the driver an address.

'Where are we going?'

'To my apartment.'

'There is no way under the sun that I am going to your apartment, Riccardo!' The prospect of being somewhere with him on her own, without the protection of other people around, sent her nervous system skittering into mad overdrive.

'Oh, yes, you are.' He shot her a sideways glance and said unevenly, 'We need to talk.'

'We've already done that!'

Why should she be interested in going over old ground? How many more times did she have to hear that he wanted her and that she should capitulate? How many more times did she have to listen to him tell her that the physical attraction that burned through their bodies like hot lava was just too big to resist?

'No, we haven't. At least, I haven't.'

There was something uneven in his voice that made her stare at him, but he wasn't looking at her and her heart was slamming against her ribcage as they completed the remainder of the short drive in tense silence.

'I won't lay a finger on you, Julia,' he said as they took the lift up to his apartment. Surprisingly, he still wasn't looking at her and she felt a little flutter of dreaded excitement stirring in her blood. 'I just want to...talk.'

She followed him docilely into his apartment, only vaguely registering the classic minimalist styling of the confirmed bachelor. A bachelor wealthy enough to have the best of everything, but without the desire to improve on any of it. The entire apartment was wooden-floored, with a sunken sitting area to one side that was lavishly furnished with a black leather sofa and two chairs. The kitchen was open-plan and looked brand-new, as though the various appliances had never been touched.

He was walking now towards a bar area that was an

exquisite blend of various woods, so smoothly joined together that it appeared as if they were all from the same tree.

'Well, now that you've got me here, what do you want to talk to me about?' She dared not go any closer to him, so she remained where she was in the middle of the vast, open-plan room, clutching her little black handbag in both hands.

He poured himself another whisky, offering her a drink, which she refused with a shake of her head, and then moved to the leather sofa, where he sat down, leaning forward with his arms resting on his thighs and his head lowered.

He couldn't remember a time when he had been nervous. Not even when he had sat his exams in his youth, or taken his driving test. Certainly never in the company of a woman. He was nervous now. He could feel it racing through his veins like deadly adrenaline and his breathing was shallow and laboured.

He was only aware that she had approached him when he saw the black high-heeled shoes out of the corner of his eye. He waited until she had hesitantly sat on the sofa next to him, and even then he didn't dare look her in the face.

'What's the matter?' she asked in a hushed voice. She was so accustomed to his towering self-control, his confident assumption that other people were born to fall in line with his wishes, that to see him like this now was throwing her into a state of inner turmoil.

'Why did you come to the restaurant, Riccardo? What…what have you got to talk to me about?'

He finally looked at her, his black eyes shorn of their self-assurance. Julia felt her heart flip over and shakily told herself that this was all just another ploy to get her into his bed. He wasn't ready to forgo his challenge, he had simply decided to switch tactics, to get her to somehow feel sorry for him so that he could move in on her vulnerability. It didn't quite ring true, but she braked at the possibility of speculating further.

'I came to the restaurant because I had to. I had no option. I told myself that you could see whoever you wanted to see, that you were free to do whatever you wanted, but I realised that I do not want you to be free. I do not want you to see other men, to talk to other men or even to think about other men. I sat down in front of my work papers and all I could see was you and that man, laughing, talking, going back to his place, making love. I came because I was torn apart with jealousy.' He raked his fingers through his hair and then pressed the palms of his hands tightly against his eyelids.

Julia felt herself begin to melt. If this was a ploy then it was working. She could never be without this man and to have him for only a short while would be worth the lifetime of heartache that would follow. She tentatively reached out and placed her hand on his thigh and he covered it with his hand, squeezing it gently.

'Riccardo.' She sighed and edged closer to him. 'I give up. I know you want me and I want you and I just…give up. I'll be your little fling.'

'It's not good enough.' He turned to face her fully and for a few dazzling seconds Julia was caught between bewilderment that her offer had just been refused and hope that the tender expression in his eyes would give her the answers she desperately yearned to hear. 'I don't just want your body. Oh, I fooled myself that that was all there was, but I want your soul as well.'

'What are you saying?' Julia whispered as the little seed of hope began to shoot up, swarming through her entire body until she was engulfed with it.

'I'm saying that I love you.'

'You love me?' Her eyelashes glimmered with the sheen of tears and he pulled her roughly towards him, burying his head in her hair so that his words were muffled.

'I love you,' he confirmed in a shaking voice. 'I don't know how and when it happened but you went from being the source of my rage to the object of more emotions I ever thought it was possible to have. I told myself that it was all about lust because I knew that I could control lust, that lust was transitory and did not involve the heart. I believed that one failed marriage had made me jaded towards the whole concept of love except...except when I thought about that I realised that what I felt for Caroline had never been love. I had fallen for the concept of the ideal woman. The truth was that Caroline left me cold, even before I finally admitted to myself that my marriage was dead and due a decent burial service. I clung on because of pride but now I realise that the best thing she ever did was to find someone else, someone who could restore her faith in human nature. But still, I stupidly tried to convince myself that there was no such thing as love. Then I told myself that I would seduce you as some warped form of punishment for dropping a bombshell in my life, and when that didn't work I said that I was just doing it because you were a challenge. But I wasn't. I wanted you because somewhere along the line I fell in love with you.'

'Oh, Riccardo.' Her voice broke then and she tilted her face to his and gently kissed his lips. 'Do you mean it? Mean it all?'

'Every word,' he said in a choked voice.

'I could never understand how you could possibly be attracted to me when all your ex-girlfriends had looked like Helen Scott...'

'Because love runs deeper than looks. You are not just

beautiful on the outside, my dearest darling, you are beautiful on the inside as well. Why do you think that when I was in your company I could never tear my eyes away from you, and when you were not around my mind was filled with you? You made every emotion I ever felt pale into insignificance…

'I know you have doubts about me,' he continued gruffly, 'but—'

'No doubts.' Julia smiled, filled with bliss and wonder that this big, dark, powerful man cradling her against his chest could actually love her. 'You have no idea how much I've wanted you to tell me what you just did. I fell in love with you and it hit me like a bolt from the blue. When you kept talking about want I felt that I had to run away because I wanted so much more from you.'

'And that's why you accepted a date with that wimp…'

'Roger is not a wimp!' Julia smiled with unconcealed pleasure into his chest. 'Although I did find my attention straying quite a bit when I was sitting at that table with him.'

'Straying to me, I take it?'

Julia moved sinuously against him, curling into his body, and he groaned. 'Carry on like that and my little talk for the night is finished,' he growled, bending to kiss her with a fierceness that was returned.

'Oh, good.' She began unbuttoning his shirt, running her hands over his broad chest and teasing the flat brown nipple with her finger. 'Just so long as you take it up again later.'

'Later,' he promised solemnly, 'and tomorrow and the day after, right into forever…'

EPILOGUE

'APPARENTLY you're the woman for me,' Riccardo said, his arm around Julia's shoulders as they both sat on a swinging chair on the wooden deck, staring out into the velvet moonlit darkness. She could hear the sound of the surf, gently lapping against the beach ahead of them, although the sea was just a black lake, fringed with sand and the swaying trees.

'It would seem that I need a woman who can keep me on my toes.' He tilted his bottle of beer, swallowed a mouthful and leant to nuzzle the neck of the woman he adored.

'And I thought your daughter was the one who could do that,' Julia murmured with a smile on her face. Nicola was absorbed with her father, but she would never forget her mother. Neither she, Julia, nor Riccardo would allow that to happen.

'Oh, that child of mine can keep anyone on their toes. I needn't tell you that my family think the world of her. The first granddaughter among four grandsons. She will be spoilt rotten.'

They had been in Italy for two weeks now and Julia had met most of his family and it was as vibrant and closely knit as he had promised. She had been afraid that her mother might have been put off by the sheer volume and effervescence of them all, but she had taken to them like a duck to water.

'And what about the next child?' She patted her stomach which was only now beginning to show the signs of the baby she was carrying, the baby that had been conceived when love had still been an unmentionable word and passion had driven caution to the winds.

'A son,' Riccardo said firmly and he laughed that sexy, low laugh of his that never failed to make the hairs on the back of her neck stand on end. 'I shall need all the help I can get to support me with my women…'

He placed his hand over hers on her stomach and then began stroking her belly in slow, circular movements until her body went limp and she moaned softly under her breath.

'I absolutely refuse to make love out here,' she said, hooking her finger around his thumb. 'Nicola might be sound asleep, but mothers have a tendency to hear the smallest of sounds. My mum would have a heart attack if she came out here and found us…'

'In flagrante delecto…?' He chuckled. 'Your mum would discreetly disappear with a smile on her face. You know I can do nothing wrong in her eyes.'

'Poor, deluded woman…' Julia turned to kiss him, holding his beautiful face between her hands. 'However, there is the beach, and it is rather warm tonight…'

'You're a wicked woman.'

'My darling, you taught me everything I know…'